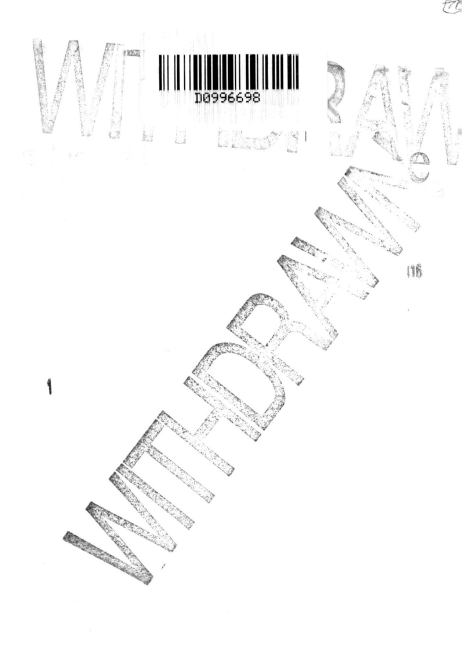

D0996698

116

For the longest time, he said nothing.

Demanded no explanations.

He simply held her and let her cry, and if Pip hadn't realised she was in love with this man before, she could have no doubt about it now. He had no idea what she was so upset about, but he was still prepared to hold and comfort her. It was like the way he accepted Alice as part of her life. Whoever she was and whatever baggage she brought with her was made to feel acceptable.

And when she was finally ready to talk, he listened with the same kind of attentiveness with which he had heard the story of her past. He held her as she spoke, and every subtle movement of his body and hands implied willingness to be there. To support her.

Pip turned her face and received his kiss, this time on her lips. It was a kiss that carried all the strength of passion and yet there was nothing overtly sexual about it. It was like nothing Pip had ever experienced. More than sex. More than friendship. It conveyed hope. The possibility that Toni had fallen in love with her to the same degree she had with him.

Alison Roberts lives in Christchurch, New Zealand. She began her working career as a primary school teacher, but now juggles available working hours between writing and active duty as an ambulance officer. Throwing in a large dose of parenting, housework, gardening and pet-minding keeps life busy, and teenage daughter Becky is responsible for an increasing number of days spent on equestrian pursuits. Finding time for everything can be a challenge, but the rewards make the effort more than worthwhile.

Recent titles by the same author:

A FATHER BEYOND COMPARE*
ONE NIGHT TO WED*
EMERGENCY BABY*
THE SURGEON'S PERFECT MATCH
THE DOCTOR'S UNEXPECTED PROPOSAL†

Specialist Emergency Rescue Team
†*Crocodile Creek: 24-Hour Rescue*

THE ITALIAN DOCTOR'S PERFECT FAMILY

BY
ALISON ROBERTS

MILLS & BOON®
Pure reading pleasure

First published in Great Britain 2007
Large Print edition 2007
Harlequin Mills & Boon Limited,
Eton House, 18-24 Paradise Road,
Richmond, Surrey TW9 1SR

© Alison Roberts 2007

ISBN: 978 0 263 19376 3

Set in Times Roman 16½ on 19¾ pt.
17-1207-48079

Printed and bound in Great Britain
by Antony Rowe Ltd, Chippenham, Wiltshire

THE ITALIAN DOCTOR'S PERFECT FAMILY

CHAPTER ONE

THE nudge from a small elbow demanded attention.

'Pip?'

Philippa Murdoch turned her head swiftly. 'Sorry, hon—I was miles away.'

In the emergency department, no less, where she'd had to leave a patient who hadn't been overly impressed by the disappearance of his albeit junior doctor.

'I think they're calling me.'

'Alice Murdoch?'

Everyone in the packed waiting room of the paediatric outpatient department was looking at each other with a vaguely accusatory air. Maybe they'd all had the same kind of hassle as Pip in fitting in their appointments and they didn't appreciate the possibility of further delay due to a less than co-operative patient.

'Here!' Pip stood up hurriedly, wishing she'd left her white coat downstairs. The woman who'd been trying to negotiate a truce between three small children fighting over the same toy in the corner gave her a suspicious look that made her feel as though she was somehow jumping the queue by means of professional privilege.

As if! They'd probably waited as long as anybody here for an appointment with the most popular paediatrician in the city. Which was why Pip had been forced to abandon her own duties to make sure the consultation wasn't lost.

Had she missed something in that initial assessment of her last patient? The symptoms had been non-specific and unimpressive and too numerous to find one that seemed significant, but maybe she should have taken more notice of that toothache he'd mentioned? What if Pip had left him under observation while he was busy having a heart attack? She should have ordered a twelve-lead ECG and some bloods rather than more routine vital sign observations.

She and Alice were ushered into a small room with three chairs in a triangle on one side of a desk and a couch against the opposite wall. The nurse deposited a plain manila folder with Alice's name on the front onto the desk.

'Have a seat,' she invited. 'Dr Costa won't be long.'

Alice raised her eyebrows. 'Funny name, isn't it?'

'It's Italian.'

'Why can't I just go back to Dr Gillies?'

'Dr Gillies is our family doctor. Part of his job is to get someone else to see his patients if he's not sure what's wrong. It's called referral.'

Alice absorbed the information with a small frown. Then her face brightened.

'Knock, knock,' she said.

'Who's there?' Pip responded obligingly.

'Dr Costa.'

'Dr Costa who?'

'Dr Costa lotta money.'

Pip's grin faded with astonishing rapidity as

she realised she wasn't the only one to have heard Alice's joke, but the tall, dark man, whose sudden presence seemed overwhelming in the small consulting room, was smiling.

'I don't really cost much at all,' he said to Alice as he eased his long frame into the remaining empty chair and leaned forward slightly. 'I'm free…and I'm all yours.'

Alice was staring, open-mouthed, and Pip could sympathise with the embarrassed flush creeping into the girl's cheeks. She would have been thoroughly disconcerted to have a dose of masculine charm like that directed at *her*. Poor Alice would have no idea how to respond.

The soon-to-be-teenage girl was currently the sole focus of attention from a man who had to be far more attractive than any one of the pictures of the movie-star and pop idols that Alice and her friends already enjoyed discussing at length.

With hair and eyes as dark as sin, a killer smile and that intriguing accent, it was no wonder that one of the senior ED nurses had sighed longingly when Pip had explained the necessity of accompanying Alice to this appointment.

'I wouldn't miss that opportunity myself.' Suzie had laughed. 'In fact, I wonder if I could borrow someone's kid?'

'It's only because my mother's got some kind of horrible virus that's making her vomit and Alice is too young to go by herself.'

'It's not a problem,' Suzie had assured her. 'Your voluble Mr Symes has probably only got a virus as well. I'll keep a close eye on him while you're gone.' She waved Pip towards where Alice was waiting patiently on a chair near the door. 'Go. Enjoy!'

And with that smile from Dr Costa now coming in her own direction, it was impossible not to feel a curl of very feminine pleasure. Philippa could hear an echo of Suzie's sigh somewhere in the back of her head as she returned the smile.

'And you must be Alice's…sister?'

The noticeable hesitation was accompanied by a spark of curiosity in those dark eyes, but who wouldn't wonder about such an obvious age gap between siblings? There was also a subtle frown that suggested the doctor was puzzled by the somewhat unorthodox situation of a sibling accompanying a new patient to a medical consultation.

That inward curl shrivelled so fast it was a flinch, but Pip managed to keep her smile in place for another heartbeat. About to correct his assumption, she was interrupted by Alice.

'Mum's sick,' Alice informed Dr Costa. 'Isn't she, Pip? She couldn't come with me today 'cos she's got some horrible bug that's making her throw up all the time.'

'I'm sorry to hear that!'

He really sounded sorry, too. Pip took a deep breath.

'We didn't want to miss this appointment.' She didn't need to catch the meaningful glance from Alice that pleaded with her not to make any corrections. It could be their secret, couldn't it? Dr Costa wasn't the first person to assume they were sisters and it was much cooler than reality as far as Alice was concerned.

It seemed perfectly reasonable. Secrets were fun after all, and if they were harmless, they only added to bonds between people.

'There's quite a waiting list to get into one of your clinics, Dr Costa,' Pip added calmly, as she shot Alice just the ghost of a conspiratorial wink.

'Call me Toni. Please.' He was eyeing her white coat. 'You're on staff here, Pippa?'

'It's Pip. Short for Philippa.' Though she liked *Pippa* rather a lot more, especially delivered with that accent. 'And, yes, I've just taken up a registrar position here. I'm a month into my run in the emergency department.'

Alice was watching the exchange with keen interest.

'I thought you were supposed to be Italian,' she said to her doctor.

'I am. I come from Sardinia, which is a big island off mainland Italy.'

'Tony doesn't *sound* very Italian.'

'It's Toni with an "i",' she was told. 'Short for Antonio. Will that do?'

Alice returned the smile cautiously. 'I guess.'

It was Pip's turn to receive another smile. 'Thank goodness for that. What would I have done if I couldn't have established my credentials? Now…' He reached for the manila folder on the desk. 'Tell me, Alice, how is it that you've come to see me today?'

Alice looked puzzled. 'I came on the bus from school. I often do that now so that Pip can give me a ride home in her car. I used to have to catch *two* buses.'

Pip caught the unspoken appeal as the paediatrician opened the file. He wasn't getting the short cut he might have hoped for in this consultation.

'Alice's GP made the referral,' she said helpfully. 'He's been trying to find a cause for recurrent abdominal pain with associated nausea and vomiting and some general malaise that's been ongoing for several months now.'

Toni Costa was nodding as he skimmed the referral letter. 'No evidence of any urinary tract infections,' he noted aloud, 'but your doctor's not happy to settle for a diagnosis of childhood migraine or irritable bowel syndrome.'

'Mmm.' Actually, it had been Pip who hadn't been happy to settle for an umbrella diagnosis, but she didn't want to have anyone else thinking she was interfering because of her training.

The swift glance she received from her senior

colleague conveyed a comprehension of her thought that was instant enough to be unsettling, but his expression suggested a willingness to respect her opinion that Pip appreciated enormously. The invitation to say more was irresistible.

'Mum had a cholecystectomy for gallstones a few years ago,' she told Toni. 'And she had an episode of pancreatitis last year. The symptoms were rather like what Alice seems to experience.'

Pip paused, waiting for the kind of reaction Dr Gillies had made to the suggestion. The unsubtle query of how soon after Shona's illness Alice's symptoms had appeared. As though Alice was disturbed enough to be suffering from Munchausen's syndrome and had latched onto a known condition. As if you could fake the symptoms like tachycardia and pallor and vomiting that could come with real, severe pain!

'And you're concerned about a possibility of an hereditary condition?'

'Yes.' The tension in Pip evaporated. Toni Costa

was going to take her concerns seriously. Her opinion of this man shot up by several notches.

'What's a hairy-de-tairy thing?' Alice demanded. She gave Pip a suspicious glare. 'You never said I might have *that*.'

Toni was smiling…again, and Pip decided that was just the way his face naturally creased all the time. Did smiling always make those almost black eyes seem to dance? No wonder he was so popular with his patients.

'Hereditary just means it's something you were born with,' he was explaining to Alice. 'You get a whole parcel of genes when you born and some of them come from your parents and grandparents and something hereditary means it came in the parcel.'

'Is it bad?'

Toni shook his head, making sleek waves of rather long, black hair move. 'It doesn't mean anything by itself, Alice. It's like catching one of your buses. If it's hereditary it just means you already had your ticket. If it isn't, you're buying the ticket when you jump on the bus instead. It's the bus we're interested in, not the ticket.'

Was he always this good at explaining things to children? Further impressed, Pip watched the satisfied nod that made Alice's ponytail bounce.

'So what's my bus, then?' she asked. 'Where's it going to take me?'

'That's what we're going to try and find out.' Toni Costa folded his hands on his lap and leaned forward a little. 'Tell me all about these sore tummies you've been getting.'

It was a relief to slide into a routine initial assessment of a new patient. Toni could now completely ignore the slightly odd atmosphere in his consulting room.

'And how often do you get the sore tummy, Alice?'

The young girl screwed up her nose thoughtfully. 'The last time was the same day as Charlene's party because I couldn't go.'

'And how long ago was that?'

'Um...well, it's Jade's party this weekend and she's exactly a month older than Charlene.'

'Older?'

'I mean younger.'

Toni nodded. 'So the last episode was a month ago. And the one before that?'

'I had to miss school and they were going on a trip to the art gallery that day.'

Toni raised an eyebrow at Alice's sister and could see the smile in her eyes. She had to know exactly what it was like, chasing the information he required, and how frustrating the process could be sometimes.

'They're happening at four-to-six-week intervals,' she supplied readily. 'And it's been ongoing for nearly six months now.'

With a quick, half-smile by way of thanks, Toni turned his attention back to his patient. 'It must be annoying to miss special things like your friends' parties,' he said sympathetically.

'Yes,' Alice agreed sadly. 'It really is.'

'So the pain is quite bad?'

'Yes. It makes me sick.'

'Sick as in *being* sick? Vomiting?'

'Sometimes.'

'Is the pain always the same?'

'I think so.'

'How would you describe it?'

The girl's eyes grew larger and rounder as she gave the question due consideration. Pretty eyes. A warm, hazel brown with unusual little gold flecks in them.

Her sister had eyes like that as well. Very different.

Intriguing.

Toni cleared his throat purposefully. 'Is it sharp?' he suggested helpfully into the growing silence. 'Like someone sticking you with a big pin? Or is it dull, like something very heavy sitting on you?'

Alice sighed. 'Kind of both.'

Toni gave up on getting an accurate description for the moment. 'Is it there all the time or does it go away and then come back—like waves on a beach?'

'Kind of both,' Alice said again. She bit her lip apologetically and then tried again. 'It doesn't really go away but it gets worse and then not so worse.' She shook her head. 'It's really hard to remember.'

'I know, but it's important you tell me everything you can remember about it. Does it stay in one place?'

'Yes. In my tummy.' Alice gave him a long-suffering and eloquent look. Did he really expect a tummy pain to go somewhere else—like her head, maybe?

Toni smiled. 'What I meant was, does it stay in *exactly* the same place? Does it get bigger and go to more places in your tummy, or does it make your back feel sore?'

Alice's face brightened. 'Sometimes it helps if I put the hottie on my back instead of my front. Is that what you mean?'

'Yes. Knowing that sort of detail is very helpful.'

Radiation of abdominal pain to the back could well point to something like pancreatitis and the thought automatically took Toni's gaze back to the older woman sitting in front of him.

She had to be quite a lot older than her sister. Late twenties probably, which was why he had been initially hesitant in querying their relationship to each other. Far better to assume they were siblings than to insult a woman by suggesting she looked old enough to be someone's mother.

The resemblance was certainly marked enough to make them believable siblings. Pip had those

same astonishing eyes. Her hair was a lot darker—
a real chestnut instead of red-gold—but the genetic
inheritance in the soft waves was also apparent.

And should be of no interest whatsoever in
this interview.

'Any associated symptoms other than the
vomiting?' he found himself asking steadily.
'Diarrhoea, headache, temperature?'

Pip shook her head.

'And no family history of migraine?'

'No.'

'Peptic ulcers? Gastrointestinal reflux?'

'No. And she's been trialled on antacid medications.'

'Any unusual stress factors or family circumstances?'

Pip looked startled. Almost taken aback.

How curious.

'I don't have an ulcer,' Alice said firmly.
'That's silly. Only old people get ulcers. They
thought Nona might have one once.'

'Nona?'

'Mum's name is Shona,' Pip put in quickly.
'For some reason, that's what Alice started

calling her when she learned to talk, and it stuck.'

'Oh?' The extra distraction from professionalism was unavoidable. 'How strange!'

Pip's gaze was shuttered and her tone guarded. 'Is it?'

'Only to me, maybe.' Toni smiled reassuringly. 'I was largely brought up by my grandmother. Nonna.'

'Was *her* name Shona, too?' Alice sounded fascinated. 'How weird!'

Toni shook his head. 'No. *Nonna* is Italian for grandmother.'

And that was more than enough personal stuff. So odd that sharing something so private had seemed compelling. Almost as odd as the glance now passing between the Murdoch sisters. Toni stood up in an attempt to get completely back on track.

'Now, *cara*, it's time I had a good look at this tummy of yours. Can you climb up onto the bed for me?'

But Alice was staring at him now. 'Why did you call me Cara? My name's Alice.'

'Sorry, it's Italian. It means...sweetheart.'

'Oh...' Alice dropped her gaze shyly as she moved to climb onto the examination couch. 'That's all right, then.'

There weren't many people that could have won Alice Murdoch's full co-operation so easily. Pip stayed where she was, seated by the desk, while Toni began his examination. Close enough for support but far enough away to allow closer interaction between doctor and patient. Pip was more than happy to observe an examination that was thorough enough to be both impressive and a learning experience for her. She would make sure she remembered to apply the same principles for her next paediatric patient.

Toni did a head-to-toe check of Alice with astonishing efficiency, covering a basic neurological, cardiovascular and respiratory assessment before concentrating on Alice's abdomen. He also fired questions at Pip. Fortunately, the focus of his attention and the distance across the consulting room meant he probably didn't notice anything unusual in her responses.

But, then, he wouldn't be expecting her to be able to answer them easily, would he?

'Do you know if there were any difficulties associated with Alice's birth and the pregnancy?'

'Ah...' Pip had to stifle a kind of incredulous huff of laughter. 'Difficulties' couldn't begin to cover the emotional and physical trauma of a sixteen-year-old girl discovering she was pregnant.

Having the father of that baby abdicate any kind of responsibility or even acknowledgement of his child.

Being forced to burden her own mother who was still trying to get her life back together after the tragic loss of her husband and Pip's father only the year before.

Suffering a labour that had been so badly managed, prolonged and horrendous that Pip had known ever since that it was an experience she could never face repeating.

Her hesitation was interpreted as a negative response, but Toni's nod indicated it was only to be expected. 'I imagine you would have known if there had been anything seriously amiss.'

'Yes, I think I would have.'

'Normal milestones?' he asked, after listening to Alice's chest and heart with a stethoscope. 'Do you remember what age Alice started walking, for instance?'

'She was just over twelve months old.'

Twelve months that had been the hardest in Pip's life. The responsibility and practical skills of caring for a baby would have been totally overwhelming and dreadful if it hadn't been for Shona. In a way, though, it had been a wonderful twelve months because Shona had forged an even closer bond with her daughter and then rediscovered her joy in life through her granddaughter. That she had become more of a mother to Alice than Pip had been gradual but inevitable as Pip had been encouraged to finish her schooling and even chase her dream of going to medical school.

'What about talking?' Toni asked, as he let down the pressure from the blood-pressure cuff around Alice's arm.

'I'm not so sure about that. Around two, two and a half.' Hard to confess her lack of certainty but it was true—she wasn't sure. Alice hadn't been stringing more than a few single words together when Pip had headed away for her first term at university, but she had been chattering by the time she'd headed home for her first holiday break.

'Childhood illnesses? Measles, mumps, chickenpox and so on?'

'She's fully vaccinated. She had chickenpox when she was…oh, about four. The whole kindergarten class came down with it, I seem to remember.'

Not that Pip had been there to help run baths with soothing ingredients or apply lotion or remind Alice not to scratch. The letters and phone calls from her mother had made her feel guilty she hadn't been there to help and share the worry. Worse than the poignancy of missing the joy of other milestones. But, as Shona repeatedly said, it wasn't because she didn't love Alice. She was doing what was best for both of them. For their futures. It couldn't be helped that she had to be away so much.

No wonder their relationship worked so much better as sisters now. They all knew the truth, of course, but it worked so well for all of them the way it was.

Pip had the niggling feeling that Dr Toni Costa might not think it was an ideal arrangement. He already thought it strange that Alice called her mother 'Nona' and there had been something hidden in the tone which with he'd shared the information that he'd been raised by his grandmother. She wasn't about to try and analyse why she didn't want to be thought less of by Alice's paediatrician but it was enough to prevent her correcting his initial assumption that was now making answering his questions rather uncomfortable.

It was a relief when he concentrated totally on Alice again for a few minutes.

'Show me where you feel the pain in your tummy.'

Alice pointed vaguely at her midriff.

'Does it hurt if I press here?' His hand was on the upper middle portion of Alice's abdomen.

'A little.'

Pip could see how gentle he was being, however. How sensitive his touch was. It was hard to look away from that hand, in fact. The olive skin with a dusting of dark hair. Long fingers and neatly manicured nails. Movements that were confident but careful.

'What about here?' He was trying the upper right quadrant now. The area that pain would be expected if Pip's suspicions had any grounds.

'Yes,' Alice said quickly. 'That hurts.'

'A little or a lot?'

'Not too much. But that's where it gets *really* sore when I get sick.'

The strident beeping at that point made Toni glance at the pager clipped to his belt. Then he raised his eyebrows in Pip's direction.

'Sorry. I think ED's trying to contact me.'

'Feel free to use the phone on the desk if you wish.'

'Thanks.' Pip was embarrassed to interrupt the examination but she couldn't not take the call. What if her Mr Symes was busy having a cardiac arrest in a side room or something?

Suzie sounded apologetic as well. 'I'm sure it's nothing, but Mr Symes is complaining of chest pain now. Says it's a crushing, central pain that's radiating to his left arm.'

Classic symptoms. Almost too classic. 'Any associated symptoms?'

'Not really. He's been complaining of nausea since he came in, along with all those aches and pains, but he's not vomiting or sweating or anything. He reckons this came on suddenly.'

'I don't suppose he gave you a pain score without being asked, did he?'

Suzie laughed. 'Ten out of ten. Do you think he's been reading the right textbooks?'

'We can't afford to make assumptions. Can you do a twelve-lead ECG and put him on telemetry?'

'Sure.'

'What's his blood pressure?'

'One-fifty over ninety.'

'Safe to try a dose of GTN, then. Put him on oxygen as well. Six litres a minute.'

'OK.'

'We'll do some more bloods, too, and add in cardiac enzymes. I can do that when I come down. I shouldn't be much longer.'

In fact, Toni was sitting down to share his findings with her as she hung up the phone, and

Pip was aware of a vague feeling of disappointment that the consultation was almost over.

'Cardiac patient?' he queried.

'Probably not, but we'll have to rule it out.'

'I won't keep you too long. Alice seems like a normal, healthy little girl on first impression. The only finding I can make is mild and rather non-specific abdominal tenderness.'

That feeling of disappointment grew. Were her instincts misplaced? And would there be no reason for Alice to see Dr Costa again?

'Mind you, that's not an unexpected result and it certainly doesn't mean I don't wish to make any further investigations.'

Pip nodded, listening intently.

'I'd like to do some further blood tests and another urine culture and microscopy. I think a general abdominal ultrasound examination would be a good idea. Maybe even an MRI scan.' Toni was ticking boxes and scribbling notes on request forms.

'We might like to consider a carbon-labelled urea breath test and possibly endoscopy to rule out the gastritis and duodenal ulceration that *Helicobacter pylori* can cause.'

Pip nodded again. This was more than she had expected.

'Alice hasn't been hospitalised with any of these episodes, has she?'

'No. I came close to bringing her in the first time because she was so miserable, but it only lasted about half an hour.'

'It would be ideal if we could see her and get a blood sample while she was having the pain. To check liver function for elevated blood amylase levels.'

'So you think pancreatitis is a possibility?' Pip caught Toni's gaze and held it. To voice the unthinkable—that Alice could have a tumour of some kind—was unnecessary. The eye contact told her that he already knew her deepest fear.

'I'm not ruling anything out at this stage. We'll find out what's causing the problem and then we'll deal with it, yes?'

'Yes.' Pip dropped her gaze, embarrassed to show how grateful she was. 'Thank you.'

'And you'll bring her in if it happens again?

And call me? I'd like to see her myself if it's at all possible.'

The warm smile that curled around the words made Pip think that this consultant might even get out of bed and come into the hospital at 3 a.m. if that's when the attack happened to occur.

And that he was really going to do whatever it took to make a diagnosis and then fix whatever was wrong with Alice.

Did all the relatives of his patients feel so cared about?

So…safe?

Pip was smiling back as Alice finished getting dressed and plopped into the chair beside her. She glanced from Toni to Pip and then back again.

'OK,' she said. 'Where's my bus off to, then?'

Alice was less than impressed with all the tests she might have to undergo.

'Why can't they just take an X-ray or something? You know I *hate* needles.'

'An ultrasound test is completely painless and it's better than an X-ray. And an MRI scan is even better. It's like having photographs taken of what's inside your tummy. It's incredibly detailed.'

'Ooh, gross! Can you see, like, what you had for breakfast?'

Pip laughed. 'Almost, but I wouldn't worry about any of it. You might have to wait for weeks to get an appointment for something like an ultrasound. We'll do what Dr Costa suggests and bring you into hospital next time you get a sore tummy.'

'Will you come with me?'

'Of course.'

'What if you're working?'

'Then I'll stop working to look after you. Like I did today to go to your appointment.'

'Do you get into trouble for doing that?'

'Of course not.' Pip almost managed to convince herself as well as Alice. 'I just have to make up for it later. Like now. Are you OK to sit in the staffroom and read magazines while I go and look after the patients I still have?'

'Sure.'

'You can get a hot chocolate out of the machine. You know how to work it, don't you?'

'Yeah.'

They bypassed the main area of the emergency department to reach the staffroom.

'Hey, Pip?'

'Yeah?' When had she picked up Alice's speech patterns that now came so automatically?

'Dr Costa's nice, isn't he?'

'Very nice.' Her agreement was deliberately casual. What an understatement!

'Is he married?'

'I have no idea.' Liar! Pip knew as well as most women on the staff of Christchurch General that Toni Costa was single.

'Maybe you should find out.'

'Why?'

''Cos it's about time you got a boyfriend and *I* think Dr Costa's hot.'

Pip wasn't about to engage in that kind of 'girl-talk' with any twelve-year-old but most especially not her own daughter. 'I'm way too busy to fit a boyfriend into my life.'

'If you leave it too long, you'll get old and crusty and no one will want you.'

'Oh, cheers!' But Pip was grinning. 'For your information, kid, twenty-eight isn't *old*!'

They had reached the staffroom now but, as usual, Alice had to have the last word.

'Well, he likes *you*. I could tell.'

Toni sat back in his chair and sighed with relief as the shrieking toddler who had been the last patient in today's clinic was removed from his consulting room.

He eyed the pile of manila folders and patient notes on his desk and pulled a pen from his pocket. While it would be nice to escape the hospital completely and revel in the peace and quiet of his home, he never left a clinic until he'd expanded his rushed notes to make a detailed summary of each visit. It wouldn't take long.

When he got the Alice Murdoch's file, however, he found himself simply staring into space, fiddling with the pen instead of writing effi-ciently.

How long would it be before he saw the Murdoch sisters again? Not that he'd wish an episode of acute abdominal pain on Alice, of course.

He could always find another reason to visit the emergency department, couldn't he? A consult that he didn't send a registrar to do, for example.

It wasn't as though he intended to ask Pippa out or anything. Good grief, she was the relative of one of his patients.

Only the sister, though, not the mother. Did that somehow make it more acceptable?

But what would be the point of starting something that would go nowhere? He'd done that too many times already. And she was a doctor. A career-woman. Toni wasn't about to break his number-one rule. However ready he might be to find his life partner, the mother of his children was going to have to be as devoted to them as he intended to be.

As devoted as his own parents had always failed to be.

But he was going to have a career, wasn't he? Wouldn't any intelligent woman also want a career—at least part time?

Maybe this Pippa Murdoch was planning to go into general practice some time.

Part time.

Toni tried to shake off his line of thought. Tried, and then failed, to complete the task waiting for him on his desk.

There was just something about the bond between those sisters that was very appealing. It was something special. Unusual.

Her family was clearly very important to her. She had left a patient who sounded as though he could be having a heart attack to accompany Alice to the appointment, and she was concerned enough to be determined to get a more definitive diagnosis than her family doctor had supplied.

He respected that.

And there was no getting away from the fact that she was a beautiful woman.

Different.

Stunning, in fact.

Toni reached for the phone and punched in an extension number.

'Ultrasound Reception, Marie speaking.'

'Hello, Marie. It's Toni Costa here, Paediatrics.'

There was a small noise on the other end of the line. Almost a squeak.

'You'll be getting a request for an abdominal ultrasound on a twelve-year-old patient of mine, Alice Murdoch.'

'Yes?' Marie sounded keen to be helpful.

'I'd like you to let me know when you schedule the examination. If I'm available, I'd like to come and watch.'

'Really?' Marie recovered from her surprise. 'Of course, I'll let you know as soon as it's in the book. Is it urgent?'

Toni considered that for a moment. 'It's important rather than urgent,' he decided aloud. 'But it would be very nice if it could happen within the next week or two.'

And it would be very nice, albeit unlikely, if he happened to be free at the time of the appointment. That way, there was at least a chance he might see Pippa again in the not-so-distant future.

He went back to finishing his paperwork.

Quite oblivious to the half-smile that occasionally played at the corners of his mouth.

CHAPTER TWO

THE child looked sick.

Pip had gone past the mother, sitting with a boy aged about two on her lap, twice. They had been there for nearly half an hour and should have been seen before this, but a major trauma case had come in and a significant percentage of the senior emergency department staff were tied up with several badly injured patients in the main resus bays.

The department had been crazy all day. Pip currently had three patients under her care and they were all genuinely unwell. Seventy-five-year-old Elena was having an angina attack that was much worse than usual and could herald an imminent myocardial infarction. Her investigations were well under way and adequate pain relief had been achieved, but Pip was trying to keep an eye on her ECG trace as she waited for blood results to come back and the cardiology registrar to arrive.

Doris, in cubicle 3, was eighty-four and had slipped on her bathroom floor to present with a classic neck of femur fracture. The orderlies had just taken her away to X-Ray and then she would most likely need surgical referral for a total hip replacement.

Nine-year-old Jake had had an asthma attack that hadn't responded well to his usual medications and his frightened mother had rushed him into Emergency just as the victims from the multi-vehicle pile-up on the motorway had started arriving. Judging the attack to be of moderate severity, Pip had started Jack on a continuous inhalation of salbutamol solution nebulised by oxygen. She had also placed a cannula in a forearm vein in case IV drug therapy was needed, but his oxygen saturation levels were creeping up and the anxiety levels dropping in both mother and child.

Pip was about to check on Jake again and consider whether he needed admission to the paediatric ward.

Toni Costa's ward.

Seeing another child waiting for assessment made her think of Toni again, but Pip was getting quite used to that. It wasn't just Alice's fault for making that unwarranted but rather delicious suggestion that he'd been attracted to her. Pip preferred to think the explanation was because she'd been so impressed with the man as a paediatrician. How good he was with interacting with his young patients and what a good example he'd set in making such a thorough assessment of a new case. How he'd taken Pip's unspoken concerns seriously and made her feel that her daughter was in safe hands.

Toni wouldn't leave an obviously unwell child just sitting to one side of an emergency department and waiting too long for assessment because of pressure on resources, would he?

The small boy looked febrile. His face was flushed and appeared puffy. What bothered Pip more, however, was how quiet the child was. With the alien bustle of an overworked emergency department flowing past in what should have been a frightening environment, the boy was just lying limply in his mother's arms and staring blankly.

Even from several metres away Pip could see that the little boy was in respiratory distress. A small chest was heaving under a thin T-shirt…way too fast.

Pip moved towards him, pausing for a moment beside the central triage desk.

'Doris has gone to X-Ray so we've got an empty cubicle for a while. Could you find me a bed, please, Suzie? I think I should take a look at that little boy over there.'

'Oh, would you?' Suzie sounded relieved. 'That would be great. I was just going to upgrade him for an urgent assessment. He's looking a lot worse than he did when he came in.' She sent a nurse aide to find a bed in the storage area off the main corridor to the hospital. 'Put it in cubicle 3. Hopefully we'll have another free space by the time Doris comes back.'

A stretcher was coming through the double doors from the ambulance bay. Another one was lined up behind that.

'What's the history?' Pip queried briskly, before Suzie could get distracted by the new arrivals.

'Just became unwell today. Running a temperature, off his food. Family's new in town so they didn't have a GP to go to.'

'Cough? Runny nose?'

'Apparently not. Temp's well up, though—39.6 when we took it on arrival.' Suzie was moving to intercept the first stretcher. 'His name's Dylan Harris. Turns two next month.'

Pip smiled at a mother who was probably her own age. What would life be like for herself, she wondered briefly, if she had a two-year-old instead of a twelve-year-old? She certainly wouldn't be doing what she was doing now—a job she loved with a passion.

'Mrs Harris?'

'Yes...Jenny.'

'I'm Dr Murdoch.' The thrill of saying those words had never worn off. Worth all those long years of hard work and heartache. 'Follow me. We're just finding a bed so I can check Dylan for you.'

'Oh, thank goodness! I think he's getting sicker.'

The bed wasn't needed immediately. Pip carried the chair Jenny had been sitting on as she led the way to cubicle 3.

'Keep Dylan sitting on your lap for the moment, Jenny. It'll keep him happier and help his breathing as well.'

'He's started making funny noises.'

'Mmm.' Pip was listening to the soft stridor on expiration and a gurgle on inspiration with mounting alarm. 'And how long has he been dribbling like that?'

'Is he?' Jenny looked down at her son. 'I hadn't noticed. It must have started just now.'

Something that could compromise a child's airway this quickly was extremely serious and Pip already had a fair idea of what she might be dealing with. She signalled Suzie to indicate the need for assistance but the senior nurse was still occupied with a patient on an ambulance stretcher. Her apologetic wave and nod let Pip know she would do something as soon as she could. Pip reached for an oxygen mask.

'Hold this as close as you can to Dylan's face without upsetting him,' she instructed Jenny.

Pip could see the way the skin at the base of his neck was being tugged in as Dylan struggled to breathe and the retraction of his rib-cage when she lifted his T-shirt to place the disc of her stethoscope on the small chest.

An empty bed was being pushed into the cubicle behind her.

'Get me a nurse, please,' Pip told the orderly. 'Preferably Suzie, if she's available.' She took another glance at Dylan's face. 'You're being such a good boy. You're not feeling too good, are you, sweetheart?'

She got no response. Not even eye contact from the toddler. Pip looked up at Jenny.

'Has he been talking much today?'

'He hasn't said anything since we got here. He's not even crying, which is weird. He usually cries a lot. Does that mean it's not that serious?'

'Not necessarily.' Pip wasn't going to alarm Jenny by telling her that it was the quiet children that were usually most at risk. With the oxygen mask held close to his face, Dylan was leaning back on his mother's shoulder, his chin raised. The 'sniffing the air' position that indicated an instinctive method of maximising airway calibre.

'And he hasn't been coughing at all?'

'No. This came on really suddenly. He seemed fine except he wouldn't eat his toast this morning. I wondered if he might have a sore throat.' She cast a worried glance at her son. 'It's getting worse, isn't it?'

It was. Dylan's eyes drifted shut and his head drooped. Pip touched his face.

'Dylan? Wake up, love. Open your eyes.' She got a response but it wasn't enough. 'I'll be back in a second,' she told Jenny. Slipping through the curtain, Pip nearly collided with Suzie.

'Any of the consultants free at the moment?'

The nurse shook her head. 'One of the trauma cases has arrested. It's a circus in Resus.'

'I need a paediatric anaesthetist here,' Pip said. 'And we need to get Dylan to Theatre. I'm pretty sure he's got epiglottitis and his level of consciousness is dropping.'

Suzie's eyes widened. 'I'll find someone.'

'Get me an airway trolley in the meantime?'

'Sure.'

Pip could only hope that intervention could be avoided until Dylan was safely under the care of an expert anaesthetist.

'I think Dylan has something called epiglottitis,' she told Jenny a moment later. 'It's a nasty bacterial infection of the epiglottis, which is at the back of the throat. If it gets inflamed it can interfere with breathing, which is why Dylan has started making these noises.'

'What will you do?'

'We treat it with antibiotics but we have to protect the airway in the meantime. I'm going to get Dylan taken to an operating theatre if possible to have a tube put down his throat.'

'He needs an *operation*? Oh, my God!'

'Not an operation,' Pip said reassuringly. 'Not unless it's difficult to get a tube in place. In that case, it might be necessary to create a temporary external airway by—'

Suzie was back with a trolley. 'Someone's on the way,' she interrupted Pip. 'Shouldn't be long.'

It was going to be too long for Dylan. The small boy's eyes suddenly rolled and then closed. Jenny felt him go even floppier and when she moved the oxygen mask to look at her son, they could all see the blue tinge to his lips.

'Dylan?' Pip rubbed his sternum. 'Wake up!'

There was no movement to be seen. Including the chest wall. The toddler was in respiratory arrest. Pip plucked him from his mother's arms and laid him on the bed.

'Oh….*God*,' Jenny gasped. 'He's not *breathing*, is he?'

'No.' Pip was pulling on gloves and hoping she sounded much calmer than she felt. Where on earth was that consultant? 'We're going to have to put the tube in here. Could you hyperventilate him, please, Suzie?'

While the nurse used the bag mask to try and pre-oxygenate Dylan, Pip pulled the tubing from the suction kit and switched the unit on. She clipped a straight blade to the laryngoscope and picked out the smallest, uncuffed endotracheal tube from the sterile drape she had opened on the trolley.

'Hold his head for me, Suzie.' Pip peered over the blade of the laryngoscope moments later. 'Can't see a thing,' she muttered.

'Secretions?' Suzie asked.

'Yes. And the epiglottis is very swollen.'

'I'll give you some cricoid pressure.' Suzie pressed on Dylan's neck and Pip tried to take a deep breath and banish her mounting alarm. She knew how critical it was to get this airway secured and it was not going to be easy.

Jenny was sobbing loudly enough for another nurse to put her head around the curtain.

'I can't bear to watch,' the young mother gulped.

'Come with me for a moment, then,' the nurse said. 'I'll look after you while the doctors look after your little boy.'

Pip was barely aware of Dylan's mother being led from the cubicle due to her intense concentration on the urgent task, but even with the pressure on the neck, the secretions sucked away as much as possible and her best efforts, there was no way to get the tube past the obstruction of swollen tissue.

'It's no go,' Pip said tersely.

Suzie sounded just as tense. 'What do you want to do?'

Pip had to think fast. She couldn't rely on a

senior doctor arriving in time to take over. If she didn't do something herself, now, this little boy could die.

'Ventilate him again for me, Suzie.' She ripped open another kit on the trolley. 'I'm going to do a cricothyrotomy.'

Stripping off her gloves and reaching for a fresh pair, Pip had to fight a moment of pure panic as the consequences of not succeeding with this next procedure forced themselves into her mind.

Then, for some strange reason, she thought of Toni Costa.

Well, not so strange, really, because Dylan would probably end up being the paediatrician's patient.

And she had been thinking of Toni at rather disconcertingly frequent intervals over the last week anyway.

For whatever reason, Pip could almost sense his presence in the cubicle right now, and it brought an underlying confidence to her determination to succeed. So that Dr Costa would be impressed at the emergency care a patient of his had received.

Her fingers were as steady as a rock as she

palpated the cricothyroid membrane on Dylan's neck. There was no need for local anaesthetic as the child was deeply unconscious, and there was no time in any case. Pip stabilised the ring of cartilage with one hand and made a single, decisive incision with the scalpel.

Part of her brain registered the movement of the cubicle curtain and the fact that someone had entered the space and was now standing behind her. A large figure. Maybe it was Brian Jones, one of the emergency department consultants, answering her plea for back-up. She couldn't look up at this point, however, or hand over to anyone else, even if they were far more experienced.

Reversing her hold on the surgical instrument, Pip inserted the handle of the scalpel and rotated it ninety degrees to open the airway. Then she slid the tube into the incision, removing the introducer and replacing it with the tip of the suction apparatus tubing.

She attached the bag mask to ventilate Dylan and listened with her stethoscope to make sure both lungs were filling adequately with air. Then she checked for a pulse and looked up just as the curtain twitched back for the second time, allowing herself an audible sigh of relief.

A sigh that was abruptly terminated. It was Brian Jones who had just entered the cubicle, so who had been watching over her shoulder for the last few minutes? Pip's head swivelled for a second to find Toni Costa standing behind her.

'What's been happening?' Brian queried.

'Epiglottitis,' Pip informed her senior colleague succinctly. 'Respiratory arrest. Intubation failed due to the amount of inflammation.'

Dylan was making a good effort to breathe on his own now and was stirring. He would need sedation and the assistance of a ventilator urgently, but the consultant took a moment to nod with satisfaction.

'Well done, Pip' was high praise from a doctor known for being taciturn. 'Let's get him on a ventilator. Where's his family?'

'I'll find his mother,' Suzie offered.

'And I'll make sure they're ready for this young

man in ICU.' Toni moved to follow Suzie but turned a second later. 'Bravo, Pippa,' he said quietly. 'You certainly didn't need my assistance.'

Warmth from that single, unusual word of praise stayed with Pip until she ended what had been a memorably long day. When her last patient, Elena, had finally been admitted for observation in the chest pain ward and Doris was in Theatre, having her hip joint replaced, Pip took a few minutes to visit the paediatric intensive care unit. She wanted to check up on Dylan and, if she was honest with herself, she wanted to enjoy that sensation of having done something special. And if she was *really* honest with herself, the possibility of meeting Toni Costa again had to be a distinct bonus, so she was more than happy to find him talking to Jenny and a man she assumed to be Dylan's father.

'Oh...it's you!' Jenny's face lit up. 'He's going to be all right. Darling...' She turned to her husband. 'This is the doctor I told you about. The one who saved Dylan's life when he'd stopped breathing.'

'Really?' The man stepped forward and

gripped Pip's hand with both of his. 'What can I say? How can I thank you enough? It was…'

It was clearly too much to articulate further. Dylan's father was overcome by emotion.

'Sorry…' he choked out.

'It's OK,' Pip reassured him with a smile. 'I totally understand. It was a frightening experience.'

For her as well. What would Dr Costa think if he knew that he'd provided the confidence Pip had needed to succeed, even before the surprise of his genuine presence? She didn't dare look at him.

'I'm so pleased to hear Dylan's doing well,' she added.

'He's doing very well.'

Pip had to look up as the paediatrician spoke. She found herself basking in a smile she could remember all too easily.

The warmth of this man!

'And I must congratulate you again,' Toni added. 'I didn't get the chance to tell you how impressed I was with what I saw. I couldn't have managed that procedure any better myself. You did, indeed, save young Dylan's life.'

Pip had never felt so proud of herself. It had taken so much hardship to cope with the long training and compromises in her personal life to get to precisely this point, but Toni's approval and the gratitude of Dylan's parents made it all seem worthwhile. More than worthwhile.

But then Pip's gaze was caught by the sight of the young parents moving to sit with their son. They were holding hands with each other and they both used their free hands to gently touch their child. The bond between the three of them was palpable and Pip was aware of a sense of loss that took the shine off her pride. Life could be so complicated and there was no doubt that sacrifices had been made for her to get to where she was. Sometimes things got lost that could never be replaced.

'Don't look so worried,' Toni said. 'He is going to be fine.'

Pip nodded. And smiled—happy to let the paediatrician assume she had been thinking of the child they could see. The return smile gave no hint that he might have guessed her real thoughts, although his words were startling.

'How's Alice?' he queried.

Nobody could read minds that well, Pip reassured herself. 'She seems fine at the moment.'

'Have you received the appointment for the ultrasound examination?'

'Yes, it's next Thursday. Faster than I would have expected.'

Toni didn't seem surprised but then his attention was being diverted by a nurse approaching with a patient's chart.

'Could you sign off these medication adjustments, please, Dr Costa?'

'Sure.' But Toni was still looking at Pip as she turned away with a nod of farewell. 'I'll try and drop by to see what they find on ultrasound. Ten o'clock, isn't it?'

Pip's nod slowed and she left the unit feeling oddly dazed. How on earth had Toni known the time of the appointment? And why would he want to interrupt what had to be a gruelling work schedule in order to attend?

For one, extremely disconcerting, moment, Pip thought that maybe Alice was right. Maybe Toni Costa was attracted to her and was looking for an opportunity to see her again. She couldn't deny that the possibility of seeing *him* again had not gone unremarked in her decision to follow up on Dylan Harris's progress.

How would she feel if that *was* the case? Pip walked through the hospital corridors barely noticing the people or departments she passed. If the tingling sensation in her body right now, coming in rather pleasurable waves, was anything to go by, she would feel very good about it.

Very, very good!

Alice was not feeling very good. Pip entered her home that evening to find her daughter looking downright mutinous.

'Nona's taken my phone,' she announced by way of greeting for Pip. 'It's not *fair*!'

'It's perfectly fair.' Shona appeared in the kitchen doorway. 'You spend half your life texting your friends. You'll get it back when you've finished your homework.' She smiled at Pip. 'You're home, finally! Wash your hands, love, it's almost dinnertime.'

The tone Shona used to speak to both Pip and

Alice had been…well…motherly. Caring but firm. Possibly a little close to the end of a tether. Alice and Pip exchanged a glance. They both knew it would be a good idea to smooth potentially troubled waters. Alice disappeared upstairs, to at least look like she was doing some homework. Pip followed her mother to the kitchen.

'You OK, Mum?'

'I'm fine. Bit tired, I guess.' Shona pushed strands of her greying hair behind her ears as she bent to open the oven. 'It's just casserole and baked potatoes. Hope that'll do.'

'It'll be fantastic,' Pip said sincerely. How many other overworked and stressed junior registrars could bank on going home to a warm house and delicious hot meal? Or having their laundry done or messages run when time simply wasn't there for mundane chores?

But, then, how many twenty-eight-year-olds would want to be still living in their childhood home?

It wasn't that Pip resented the security and comfort of being mothered. It was just that—

sometimes—it would be nice to choose entirely for herself. To maybe sit down and chill out with a glass of wine instead of being immediately sucked into a predictable family routine.

A routine that had been the only way she could be doing what she was doing, Pip reminded herself. And look what she'd achieved today. A life saved. A family who would be only too happy to return to a normal routine. Pip gave her mother a one-armed hug as Shona stood up to place a tray of hot baked potatoes onto the bench.

'What's that for?' But Shona didn't sound displeased.

'Just because I love you,' Pip responded. She grinned. 'And because I had a great day today. I had to do a really tricky emergency procedure on a little boy, Mum. He'd stopped breathing. He could have died but he's going to be fine.'

'Well done, you!'

Shona's smile was proud but Pip could detect an undertone. 'You sure you're all right? Is that pain back again?'

'No, not really. Just a bit of an ache.'

'Have you made another appointment with Dr Gillies yet?'

'No. I'll do it tomorrow.'

'That's what you said yesterday. And last week.' Pip eyed her mother with concern. She looked a bit pale. And tired. 'Is Alice giving you a hard time about doing her homework?'

Shona smiled again. 'No more than usual. We'll get it done.'

That 'we' didn't need to include Pip, but she brushed aside any feeling of being left out. 'Anything I can do to help in here?'

'Have you washed your hands?'

'Mum, I'm twenty-eight! If I want to eat dinner with dirty hands, I'm allowed to.' Pip sighed fondly. 'OK, I'll go and wash my hands.'

'Good girl. Tell Alice to wash hers as well. Dinner will on the table in five minutes.'

Alice was brushing her hair and staring at herself in the bathroom mirror.

'Dinner in five,' Pip told her. 'Wash your hands.'

'Hey, Pip—can we watch "Falling Stars" after tea? In your room?'

'Sure.' Although half an hour of watching a gossip show about Hollywood celebrities wasn't Pip's cup of tea, time cuddled up on her double bed with Alice, watching the tiny screen of her portable television, had to be a highlight of any day. It was usually after Shona had gone to bed and often with illicit bowls of popcorn or a packet of chocolate biscuits to share.

Their time—with no parental type obligations to fill, for either of them.

Alice bolted her dinner with one eye on the kitchen clock.

'It's nearly 7.30,' she announced finally, with a meaningful glance at Pip.

'I know. I'm sorry I was a bit late today. Things got really busy.'

'"Falling Stars" is on at 7.30.'

'I know. You can go and watch it if you like, and I'll come after I've done the dishes.'

Shona was only halfway through a plateful of food she had been picking at without enthusiasm. 'Have you finished that assignment you have to hand in tomorrow, Alice?'

'I'll do it later.'

'No, you won't. You never do. You'll have to get it done before you do anything else, and that includes watching television. *Especially* watching television.'

'But it's my *favourite* programme!'

'It's a load of rubbish.'

'*Mum* said I could watch it.'

Alice only called Pip 'Mum' when she wanted to play one of the adults in her house off against the other, a habit that had formed over the last few months—ever since she had decided it was cool to call Pip by her given name.

Pip took one look at her mother's drawn face and knew it had been the wrong button to push tonight.

'Mum's right. You have to get your homework done, Alice. I'll tape the programme and we can watch it later.'

'But I want to watch it *now*! I've been looking forward to it *all* day!' Alice looked at Pip with the face of someone unexpectedly betrayed.

Shona said nothing but her lips were a tight line.

'Please, Pip?'

It was tempting to give in to that plea and

maybe negotiate a compromise, like supervising the homework being done later, but Pip could sense a disturbing undercurrent to what should have been an average family-type wrangle. Roles were being challenged.

Alice expected her support but maybe she was too used to getting her own way by pulling the 'friends' card out.

Shona expected her support as well. Pip was Alice's mother after all, and maybe Shona was feeling too tired or unwell not to play the 'mother' card.

Pip was caught in the middle but it was perfectly clear which way she had to jump.

'No,' she said firmly to Alice.

'But you *said*—'

'I know what I said, but I didn't know you hadn't done your homework.'

'Yes, you did! You heard—'

'That's enough!' Shona's fork hit the table with a rattle. 'I'm sick of this.'

Alice jumped up and stormed from the room, slamming the door behind her.

'Sorry, Mum,' Pip said into the silence that

followed. She sighed. 'I'm not very good at the parent bit, am I?'

'We're getting to the difficult stage, that's all.' Shona echoed Pip's sigh. 'I'd forgotten what it was like, living with a teenager.'

'Was I so awful?'

'No.' Shona smiled wearily and reached out to touch her daughter's hair. 'You were great.'

That touch took Pip instantly back to childhood where the gesture could have provided comfort, communicate pride or been as loving as a kiss. The love she had for her mother welled up strongly enough to bring a lump to her throat.

'I wasn't that great. Remember the fuss I made when you wouldn't let me get my ears pierced? I kept it up for a week.'

'It wasn't your ears I minded—it was the belly-button ring you wanted.'

'And what about that first rock concert I was determined to go to?'

'I seem to remember you getting your own way in the end that time. Thanks to your dad.'

They were both silent for a moment. The memory of that terrible wrench when Jack

Murdoch had died so suddenly was still painful. A period neither of them liked to dwell on. Pip skipped it entirely.

'And then I got pregnant.' She snorted softly. 'I have no idea how you coped with that so well, Mum.'

'When you have to cope, you do. That's all there is to it, really.'

'And you're still coping. Far more than you should have to at your time of life.' Pip couldn't brush aside the pangs of guilt. 'I should be taking full responsibility for Alice by now. I should have a house of my own and not make you live with all her mess and angst.'

'And how would that help while you're still finishing your training?' Shona straightened visibly in her chair. 'I wanted to do this, Pip. I still do. I want to see you settled into the career you've always dreamed of. Into a relationship, even.'

Pip rolled her eyes. 'Yeah, right! Just what every man my age wants—a woman who's still living at home and relying on her mum and a package deal with an angsty teenager thrown in.'

'Don't judge all men on what James thought. He was an idiot.'

'An idiot I wasted four years on at medical school. I'm in no hurry to go back there.'

'It might have helped if you'd told him about Alice a bit earlier.'

'Getting pregnant at sixteen isn't something I'm proud of, Mum.'

'Maybe not, but Alice should be,' Shona said quietly. 'You can be very proud of her.'

Shona's words stayed with Pip as she tidied up after dinner. They could both be proud of their girl, but the credit had to go largely to Shona for the successful upbringing of Alice. Imagine what a disaster it would have been if it had been left entirely to *her*? But she was much older now. Hopefully wiser. And it was way past time she took more of the burden from Shona's shoulders.

The silence from her daughter's room had been deafening and, having finished her cup of tea, Pip left Shona in the living room and went and tapped on Alice's door. It might be a good time to try and have a real 'mother-daughter' type talk. To start a new phase in their relationship.

'Alice?'

There was no response.

Pip tapped again and opened the door. Alice was curled up on her bed and had her face turned away from the door.

'Alice?' Pip stepped closer. She could see that Alice's arms were locked tightly around her slight body. 'We should talk, hon.'

Alice rolled and Pip saw that her face was scrunched into lines of what looked like severe pain. Reaching to smooth the hair from her forehead, Pip felt the damp skin and then Alice groaned.

'Oh, no!' Pip took hold of her daughter's wrist, knowing she would feel the tattoo of an overly rapid heart rate. 'Is it your tummy again? Why didn't you come and tell me?'

'It just started.' Alice broke into sobs. She didn't look anything like her twelve and a half years right now. She looked like a sick frightened little girl. And along with her maturity had gone any desire for a 'cool' relationship with her

mother. 'It hurts, Mummy. Make it go away…
please!'

'Right.' Pip pulled the duvet around Alice. 'Put
your arms around my neck. I'm going to carry you
to the car and then I'll take you into the hospital.'

'No-o-o!'

Shona had heard the noise. 'What's happening?'

'Tummy pain again. I'm going to take her into
Emergency.'

'Should I call for an ambulance?' Shona
asked anxiously.

'It'll be quicker if I take her.'

'I'll get the car out,' Shona offered. 'I can drive.'

'You don't have to come. It could be a long
night.'

'Of course I'm coming.'

'I don't want to go,' Alice sobbed. 'I don't
want to *move*!'

'I know, hon, but we have to. We need to do
what Dr Costa asked us to do. When you're in
the hospital you'll be able to have some
medicine that will take the pain away completely.'

Alice's arms came up to lock around Pip's neck. She braced herself to take the weight.

'You promise?'

'Yes.' Pip lifted the girl. 'I promise.'

'Will Dr Costa be there, like he said he would?'

'I don't know, hon. Let's hope so but it's late and he's probably gone home by now.'

Alice was still sobbing. 'But I *want* him to be there.'

'Mmm.' The strength of her own desire to have Toni Costa there was overwhelming. Pip had to close her eyes and try very hard to sound casual. 'Me, too.'

CHAPTER THREE

THE triage nurse took one look at Alice and sent them straight to a resus bay.

The registrar on duty, Graham, was right behind them.

'Let's get some oxygen on,' he ordered a nurse, 'and I want some vital sign baselines. What's going on, Pip?'

'This is Alice, she's twelve,' Pip responded. 'She's got acute epigastric pain radiating to her back with associated nausea and vomiting.'

'First time this has happened?'

'No. She had an appointment with Toni Costa recently because we want to find out what's causing it. He asked me to bring her in when it happened again so we could get bloods to check amylase levels.'

'Right. I'll get a line in straight away.'

But Alice jerked her hand away from the registrar. '*No*,' she said fiercely. 'I want Dr Costa.'

'He doesn't work in Emergency, love,' Graham said patiently. 'Come on, this won't hurt for more than a moment, I promise.'

'No.'

'We'll be able to give you something for that pain after I've put this little tube in your vein.'

'No!' Alice's sobs turned to a choking sound and Pip held her daughter's head as she vomited yet again. Shona took a dampened towel from the nurse, ready to wipe Alice's face.

'Sorry,' Pip said to Graham, 'but Toni did ask us to call him if we came in acutely. Alice was expecting to see him, I guess.'

'It's 9.30 p.m. Not much chance of him being in the building.'

'I know.'

Graham looked at the sobbing, unwell child on the bed and his expression revealed his reluctance to force treatment on someone who was very unlikely to be co-operative. He looked down at the IV cannula in his hand and then glanced at Pip.

'I could try beeping him—just in case.'

'Good idea.' Pip smoothed damp strands of Alice's hair back from her face. 'It's worth a try.' At least that way Alice would know they had tried to get the person she wanted to look after her. When she knew it was impossible, she might be prepared to let Pip put a line in her hand if Graham still wasn't acceptable.

She wasn't prepared for the look of surprise on Graham's face when he reappeared less than a minute later. 'He was in ICU. He's on his way down now.'

'Hear that, Alice?' Pip could allow herself to sound delighted on her daughter's behalf. 'Dr Costa's coming to see you.'

Alice hiccuped. 'Good.'

It *was* good. Better than good. Pip had no disagreement with Alice's conviction that Toni was the top of the list of desirable people to care for her. The worry that the paediatrician might have been in the intensive care unit because Dylan had taken a turn for the worse was dismissed with only a small pang of guilt. Pip's attention had to be focused much closer to home for the moment and she wanted the best for her own daughter.

Their confidence did not appear to be misplaced. Toni took over the resus bay from the moment he arrived and managed to exude an air of authority tempered with a charm that reduced the stress levels for everybody concerned. He actually managed to both reassure Alice and gain the information he wanted at the same time. Pip could see Alice visibly relax when the doctor smiled at her and patted her hand before his fingers rested lightly on her wrist.

'Heart rate?'

'One-twenty,' Graham supplied.

'Respirations?'

'Twenty-eight.'

'Temperature?' The touch on Alice's forehead was hardly necessary but Pip could see that it was appreciated. Alice closed her eyes and, just for a moment, the lines of pain on her face almost vanished.

'Thirty-seven point four.'

'Blood pressure?'

'Eighty over fifty.'

'Bit low. Postural drop?'

'We haven't tried assessing that.'

Pip was still watching quietly, enjoying the sensation of having an expert take over. As a doctor, it was a good learning experience, being on a parent's side of this equation. Her anxiety was actually receding to the point where Pip could register how impressive Toni's clinical skills were. He was able to palpate an invisible, tiny vein in Alice's forearm and then slip a small-gauge cannula into place without eliciting more than a squeak from his patient.

Worry kicked in again with his latest question, however. A drop in blood pressure from a change in posture could be serious and the paediatrician seemed to be looking for signs of hypovolaemic shock. What could Alice be bleeding internally from? A perforated peptic ulcer? Something as nasty as acute haemorrhagic pancreatitis?

'She said she felt dizzy when she had to sit in the car,' Pip told Toni as he taped the cannula into place.

'We'll get these bloods off and then I'd like

some fluids up,' Toni said to Graham. He smiled at the nurse who was holding a page of sticky labels already printed with Alice's details and hospital ID number, ready to label test tubes.

The smile was warm. Appreciative of her readiness and inviting the junior nurse to consider herself a valuable colleague. For an idiotic moment Pip actually felt something like jealousy.

'We need amylase levels, haemoglobin and haematocrit, electrolytes...' The list seemed to go on and on as the nurse plucked tubes with different coloured stoppers from the tray. 'And we want blood cultures as well,' Toni finished.

'Goodness!' Shona's eyes had widened at the mounting pile of test tubes.

That smile appeared again. 'Don't worry, Mrs Murdoch. It looks like we're taking a lot of blood but it's less than a teaspoonful in each tube.'

'Why the cultures?' Pip queried. 'Wouldn't Alice be running more of a temperature if this pain was caused by infection?'

Toni nodded. 'We still need to rule it out. We'll do a dipstick test on her urine as soon as we can as well.' The quick smile was almost a grin this time—faintly conspiratorial. 'I like to be thorough,' he confessed.

Thorough.

And gentle.

Pip watched Toni's hands as he carefully examined Alice's abdomen. She had watched him doing this once before and, unbidden, the memory had already returned more than once.

If only Alice hadn't planted that absurd suggestion of Toni as potential boyfriend material. If only Pip hadn't found herself remembering those hands and their touch in the middle of the night. Wondering how it feel to have them touching *her*.

It had been all too easy to imagine. And highly inappropriate, given the current setting, so it was easy to dismiss. It evaporated more than convincingly as Alice cried out in pain. Toni's voice was now as gentle as his touch but excited no odd tingles in Pip. Her focus was firmly on her daughter as she stepped forward to take the small, outstretched hand.

'It's OK, hon,' she said. 'I'm here.'

'I know it hurts, *cara*,' Toni added in an equally soothing tone. 'We're going to do something about that very soon. It's a bit mean, isn't it, but we need to try and find out what's causing it before we take the pain away.' He turned to the registrar who was adjusting the flow on the IV line attached to a bag of fluids. 'I think we could get some pethidine on board now.'

'Why not morphine?' It was the standard analgesic to use in situations such as this.

'There's some evidence it can cause sphincter of Oddi spasm.'

Graham nodded. He eyed Alice thoughtfully and Pip could tell he was trying to assess how much she weighed in order to calculate a dose of the narcotic. Toni picked up the hesitation as quickly as Pip did but showed none of the impatience some consultants might have displayed. Instead, he smiled at his young patient.

'Do you know how much you weigh, Alice?'

'No.'

'I'm sure Mum knows.'

There was a tiny pause as Shona blinked at being the focus of attention. 'Ah...' She flicked a puzzled gaze at her daughter. 'Actually, Pip's—'

'She's about thirty-two kilos,' Pip interrupted quickly. This was hardly the time or place to correct Toni's assumption about her relationship with Alice, was it?

'We'll start with 25-mg IV,' Toni told Graham. 'I'd like to get an abdominal X-ray and then admit Alice to the ward overnight.' His gaze found Pip. 'We'll restrict her fluid intake and make sure we get the pain under control. I want to do an arterial blood gas as well and we'll see if we can get that ultrasound done first thing tomorrow. We'll have the blood results back by then, and then we'll look at what else we need to do.'

A lot seemed to be happening with extraordinary ease as Toni calmly issued instructions and made more than one phone call. Even when everything was sorted to his satisfaction, he didn't take his leave.

'How's the pain now, Alice?'

'Getting better.' Alice smiled for the first time since they had arrived and then she yawned.

'We'll get you to bed as soon as you've had that X-ray and then you can have a proper rest. Would you like your mum to stay with you in the hospital tonight?'

Alice nodded slowly. 'Mummy?'

Pip gave no thought to the fact that she was about to let Toni learn of the deception she and Alice had allowed to occur. Or that she had complications in her life that were enough to scare most men firmly away. The only thing that mattered right now was Alice. Providing any comfort possible. She squeezed Alice's hand.

'What is it, hon?'

Toni's glance slid from Shona to Pip, a puzzled frown appearing between dark brows.

'Will you stay with me?' Alice asked plaintively. The question was clearly directed at Pip rather than Shona.

'Of course I will, chicken.'

Toni merely raised one eyebrow. 'If you'd rather have your sister stay with you, Alice, that's absolutely fine.'

'Pip's not *really* my sister,' Alice mumbled drowsily. 'She's my *mother.*'

* * *

The timing of the radiologist's arrival to take the abdominal X-ray Toni had ordered was fortunate. He could cover up his reaction to Alice's startling revelation by moving abruptly to go behind the protective glass screen in one corner of the main resus area. And then he was able to concentrate on the first results coming in from the blood tests.

Or appear to concentrate, at least. Toni was shocked, he couldn't deny it. Pip had been less than honest with him, hadn't she? Yes, he had to concede that he had made the assumption they were sisters himself, but she hadn't made any attempt to correct him, had she?

But, then, he knew that women couldn't be trusted, didn't he?

His grandmother would hold the prize of a visit from his parents over him to extract co-operation. He soon learnt, however, that the reality of the reward was so intermittent it could never be completely trusted. Or dismissed.

His mother had always been so believable in her promises that one day—soon—she would take him away with her. That they would be a real family and he would see more of the adored but shadowy figure of his father.

Promises that were never kept.

And there had been Ellen, of course. The woman he had begun to really love. The one who could have restored trust and instead had betrayed him the moment her former boyfriend had called for her to join him in his new life overseas.

Had he expected something different simply because this particular woman was so damned attractive?

If so, he was a fool.

Even more foolish was his decision to stay in the hospital a little longer, knowing that it wasn't due entirely to a desire to see Alice settled and to try and obtain a definitive diagnosis for what was causing her discomfort.

Something other than shock was also undeniable.

Curiosity.

The compulsion to watch, covertly, the way the three generations of this family interacted. To see if it bore any relevance and would thereby confer some understanding of the effects his own, less than usual upbringing had had on his life. Because, if he could understand, maybe he would be able to forgive.

And if he could forgive the two women who had created such misery, maybe he could move on. He might even be able to find what was so painfully lacking in his own life.

On first impression, it was easy enough to equate the kind of matriarchal status his grandmother had wielded within the Costa villa to the position Shona filled. She fussed around Pip with almost the same level of concern she displayed for Alice.

'I'll stay with Alice,' she told her daughter, when the X-ray had ruled out a perforating ulcer or major abdominal bleed. 'You've got work in the morning and you need your sleep.'

'There's no way I'm leaving Alice.' Pip had her arm around her mother's waist as they prepared to move Alice's bed to the paediatric ward. 'Besides, you need rest more than I do. I'm worried about you, Mum. You've got to stop trying to do everything. And you've *got* to go and see Dr Gillies. Tomorrow.'

The conversation was muted but Toni's senses were tuned to more than the verbal exchange between the two women. There was love and support there. A closeness that had never existed between his mother and her mother-in-law. Was that what made the difference?

'I'll come up to the ward with you,' he announced.

'You don't have to,' Pip responded quickly. 'I can see her settled and try to get that urine sample for testing.'

'I do have other patients I intended to check on before I leave.'

'Oh...of course.'

She sounded embarrassed, Toni decided. He hadn't meant the response as any kind of put-down but maybe the tone had been defensive because he wouldn't want her to guess the real reason for his interest. He'd never had much patience with people who could lay the blame for any lack of success in their lives at the feet of an unhappy childhood. You dealt with what life threw at you and you coped if you had any kind of strength.

Toni had that kind of strength.

Maybe Pip did as well. She wasn't exactly unsuccessful, was she? There were a set of parents in the paediatric intensive care ward right now who would be grateful for her skill for the rest of their lives. Being a single mother could be viewed as adversity but she had come through with flying colours. It was quite possible they had something very basic in common, which could explain the attraction.

Having checked on his other patients, Toni went back to the single room Alice had been allocated and once again covered his observation of Pip and her family by apparent absorption in recording his notes.

Alice seemed equally content to receive comfort from both Pip and Shona as they helped her into a hospital gown, persuaded her to provide a urine sample for analysis and then made her as comfortable as possible for the night. It was as though the child had two mothers, and there was no way Toni could relate to abundance like that.

He hadn't even had one, really.

He'd had a grandmother who'd done her duty, however inconvenient it might have been, and had never hidden her disapproval of her son's choice of wife. The number of times he'd seen his father could easily have been counted on his fingers and even Toni's mother, Elizabetta, had been a stranger. A beautiful visitor who arrived in a cloud of perfume and gifts, created extraordinary tension in the household and then left, never failing to leave behind a sensation of emptiness.

In the short space of less than two hours with the Murdochs, Toni had gained more of an impression of a family bond than he'd ever known himself. It was a compelling warmth that he was standing away from. It was like being in the rain, looking through a window to a room that was filled with firelight and laughter and the smell of something baking. Irresistible.

What made this family unit work when his own had been such a miserable failure? In both cases, the pregnancy had to have been accidental. Elizabetta would never have chosen the disruption to such a successful modelling career and Pippa—well, she couldn't have been more than in her mid-teens. She wore no wedding ring and Alice's surname was the same as her mother's and grandmother's, so presumably there was no father in the picture.

Toni watched Pip fill a glass with iced water from the jug on the bedside table. Her movements were graceful, her hands managing to look elegant even while performing such a mundane task.

The thought of her being sexually active at such a young age was distasteful and Pip must have felt his stare because she glanced up suddenly. Maybe something of what he was thinking showed on his face, which would explain why she looked away so suddenly, her cheeks flushing uncomfortably.

Except it didn't fit. Something about this woman made the thought as insulting as it was distasteful.

Toni's curiosity reached a new high point.

Had she been raped?

Involuntarily, he sucked in his breath, confused by the strong emotion the idea provoked.

Disgust? Not really. Anger? No. He watched the way Pip smoothed Alice's hair as she laid her head back on the pillow, having taken a sip of the iced water.

There was such tenderness there. The kind of caring Pip should have been shown herself. Maybe that odd emotion was, amazingly, regret that she could have been shown something so very different.

And how ridiculous was it to be imagining scenarios and feeling for somebody when he had no idea what the real story was? His voice, when he spoke, was uncharacteristically gruff.

'I'll be back in the morning. We'll arrange whatever other tests need to be done when we get the rest of the blood results.' Toni avoided meeting Pip's gaze as she thanked him, in the hope of avoiding any more disturbing sensations. He turned abruptly. 'Sleep well, Alice. Tell the nurses if your tummy gets sore again and they'll give you some more medicine.'

He found himself holding the door for Shona when she decided to take her leave at the same time.

'I'll get some sleep,' she told Pip, 'and then I'll be back first thing so you can sort things out with your working hours.'

The temptation to escort this exhausted-looking older woman to her car was something Toni tried to dampen. If he did that, he knew he might not be able to resist asking questions that would be satisfying a less than professional curiosity.

If he couldn't shake this desire to learn more of Philippa Murdoch's story, he could at least be honourable enough to find a way to do so face to face.

The summons to Toni Costa's office late the following afternoon was unexpected, and Pip was distinctly nervous as she weaved through the traffic of a busy hospital's corridors.

Her day had been broken on more than one occasion as she'd accompanied Alice to the various investigations Toni had ordered in the wake of the abnormal liver function test results. Investigations that must have been comprehensive enough to give him a good idea of what they might be dealing with.

To have called her to his office instead of

catching her in Alice's room or coming to find her in the emergency department suggested that it was something serious he wished to discuss.

He looked serious. Disconcertingly, there was almost an air of discomfort as he ushered Pip to a chair and then hooked a long leg up to perch on the corner of his desk as he reached for the set of patient notes. His first words, however, were reassuring.

'We've been able to rule out any indication of a possible tumour.'

'Thank God for that,' Pip breathed. 'I really was worried.'

Toni's smile revealed that he had shared her concern. 'We've also cleared her for liver disease, peptic ulcer and gastroesophageal reflux.'

Pip was watching his face intently. There was something he was undecided about telling her. 'Not much left to worry about, then, is there?'

'I'm happy to discharge her this afternoon.' Toni nodded. 'Theoretically, we should wait for a second occasion in which the pain and abnormal liver tests are consistent, but I'm confident that Alice has sphincter of Oddi dysfunction.'

Pip frowned as she searched her memory banks.

'It's not that common,' Toni told her. 'I'd be surprised if it's caught your attention yet.'

'It's got something to do with the flow of bile from the pancreas, hasn't it?'

Toni nodded again. 'The sphincter is a small complex of smooth muscle surrounding the bile ducts. The dysfunction is a benign, noncalculus obstruction, most commonly hypertonic. It can affect people of any age but typically it's middle-aged females, especially after cholecystectomy.' He raised an eyebrow. 'It can be hereditary.'

Pip mirrored his earlier nod, filing the information away. Was it possible that Shona had a similar condition that could explain her own episodes of abdominal pain?

'What's the treatment?' she queried. 'If this *is* what Alice has?'

'There are trials going on for medical therapy that affects smooth muscle structure like nitrates and sublingual nifedipine but, at present, the definitive treatment is endoscopic sphincterotomy with surgical therapy as back-up.'

'What about dietary modification? I know

Mum found it helpful to go very low fat and avoid alcohol when she had problems initially.'

'Alice isn't drinking alcohol yet, surely?'

'I hope not,' Pip agreed fervently, 'but you never know with teenagers these days. She's already talking wistfully about the parties some of her friends are allowed to go to.'

'But she's not allowed to go?'

'No.' Pip smiled fondly. 'Mum's always been very strict about things like that.'

There was a moment's rather thoughtful silence and Pip watched, fascinated at the play of emotion on Toni's face. Indecisiveness which looked totally uncharacteristic and then the beginnings of a smile that played at the corners of his mouth.

'And you, Pippa?' The question was spoken softly. 'Are *you* allowed to go out?'

Pip's jaw dropped a fraction. 'Excuse me?'

The hand movement Toni made was nonchalant, as though the startling query was of little importance. The intensity of the gaze Pip found herself subjected to, however, suggested something very different.

'I'm going to refer Alice to one of our paediatric surgeons, Greg Murray,' Toni said. 'He's going to look in on her and possibly have a chat to you about her management before she goes home this afternoon.'

Pip waited, her bewilderment increasing.

'Which means,' Toni continued, 'that…professionally speaking Alice isn't strictly *my* patient any longer.' He cleared his throat. 'Which also means that you, Pippa, are not—strictly speaking—the mother of one of my patients.'

She loved the way he continued to call her Pippa unless he caught himself. It went with that delicious accent that made everything he said sound somehow exotic and more interesting.

Not that she was sure what he was talking about right now. She knew what she *hoped* he might be talking about, but what kind of idiot would she appear if she was coming to a wrong conclusion? She felt obliged to say something in the short pause that followed his reasoning.

'Ah…yes. I suppose it does,' she managed lamely. 'Does it matter?'

'Oh, yes.' Toni let out an audible breath that was almost a sigh. 'I think it does matter.'

'Why?'

'Because it means I can ask you out. For a drink, perhaps. Or dinner.'

'You mean…on a *date*?' Pip felt faintly dizzy. Her blood sugar must be really low, she decided. If she'd found time to have lunch, she might have coped with something this unexpected without this peculiar physical effect.

'Yes,' Toni said calmly. 'That is precisely what I mean.'

Oh, Lord! Echoes of those fantasies Alice had stirred rushed to fill Pip's brain and she could feel herself blushing.

This had to be unprofessional on some level, surely? Should she say no?

But was it the stuff of long-forgotten teenage dreams, not to mention more recent ones? Should she say yes as decisively as possible?

In the end, neither word emerged. Pip opened her mouth and surprised both of them by saying, 'But…*why*?'

It was Toni's turn to look astonished. 'I'm sure a woman as attractive as you are doesn't need to ask such a question! You must be well used to being asked for dates.'

Well, no, but Pip wasn't about to admit to how many years it had been since someone had asked.

'I meant,' she said quickly, 'why *you* asked. I just…ah…wasn't expecting it.'

What an understatement! That look she had caught last night, well after Toni had had time to get used to the information regarding her real relationship to his patient, when they had been settling Alice in her room for the night, had been almost—and hardly surprisingly—one of something akin to disgust.

He was giving her a mildly amused look right now and Pip realised how ungracious she was being. It was probably a first for Toni Costa to have his motives for asking a woman out questioned.

But he didn't seem fazed. 'That's easy to answer,' he responded smoothly. 'You interest me, Pippa.'

His expression had an edge to it that Pip had not seen any hint of before this. An edge that had probably made many women in his past go rather weak at the knees.

His tone had the same silky, seductive quality as he added just another couple of words.

'A lot.'

CHAPTER FOUR

'A *date*!'

'You don't need to sound so surprised, Mum. I am female and single and reasonably presentable, I hope.'

'A *date*!' From the back seat of the car, Alice echoed her grandmother's exclamation with much greater evidence of approval. 'With Dr Costa? Oh…*man*!'

Pip looked over her shoulder with an it's-not-that-big-a-deal kind of expression that was supposed to deny sharing her daughter's underlying delight with the development. Alice just laughed.

'What are you going to wear?'

'I have no idea.'

'Where are you going?' Shona asked cautiously.

'Out for dinner.'

'Upmarket?'

Pip thought about that as she slowed down for a red traffic light. With his impeccably cut pinstriped suit and that elegant Rolex watch, Toni gave the impression he could be well used to expensive venues. Could she imagine him out of hours in faded denim jeans and a leather jacket? Perched on a bar stool at a casual bistro maybe? With those waves of black hair a little tousled and those long fingers curled around the stem of a wineglass?

Oh...*yes*.

Pip felt a powerful lurch of what could only be reawakening lust curling deep inside her belly. Shifting gear and pressing the accelerator to get the vehicle moving again was a rather necessary distraction. And hadn't Shona asked her a question? She dragged her wayward imagination back into line.

'I have no idea,' she repeated, 'but I don't have anything to wear in any case so I'll have to go shopping, I suppose.'

'Cool,' Alice said approvingly. 'Can I come with you?'

'I don't think so,' Shona said. 'You've just been in hospital overnight, young lady.'

'But I'm fine now.' Alice did look so much better, with colour in her cheeks and a sparkle back in her eyes. 'And that Dr Murray says that if the pain comes back, I can have that sort of operation thing and I'll be cured.'

'Hmm.' Shona didn't sound much happier. 'I still don't think gallivanting around town on a shopping spree is a sensible idea.'

'But I haven't had any new clothes for ages!'

'That is true.' Pip cast a sideways glance at her mother. Shona had always taken care of most of the shopping for Alice and there had been a few arguments recently over what was deemed suitable. Maybe this was something Pip could take over. It could prove to be enjoyable, quality 'girl time' together. 'Let's see how Alice is feeling tomorrow, Mum. It's late-night shopping and I'll have to go because the date's on Friday. You could have an evening to yourself and a bit of peace and quiet.'

'Hmm.' This time the sound indicated the suggestion might be welcome, which made Pip think of something else that might please her mother. She flicked on the indicator and pulled the car in toward a small group of shops. 'We're going to pick up some Indian or Chinese food,' she said firmly. 'No cooking tonight.'

Shopping with Alice had been an excellent idea, Pip realised when she opened the door to Toni's knock on Friday evening.

The chosen outfit had seemed a rather radical departure from normal—a skirt that clung to her hips and then swirled around her knees and a camisole top that looked far more like underwear than outerwear.

'It's what *everybody* wears now, Pip,' Alice had stated knowledgably. 'You're so old-fashioned!'

It had been a long time since Pip had taken much notice of fashion and she had been persuaded by Alice's criticism, helped considerably by finding a gorgeous jacket she could keep on to cover her bare shoulders. Pip had fully intended to keep the jacket on all evening but the look in Toni's eyes as he took in her appearance undermined that resolve.

How long had it been since she had felt this attractive? Certainly even longer ago than the purchase of any fashionable clothes.

A slight awkwardness prevailed when Toni accepted the polite invitation to come inside for a minute while Pip collected her handbag, but maybe she was the only one to sense the approval—excitement even—radiating from both her mother and her daughter.

An excitement that Pip was trying, very hard, not to catch. This was merely a first date after all. She would be stupid to read anything more into it than an interest.

A mutual interest.

How sad that that was enough to spark something like excitement.

Hope, even, if she was really honest with herself.

A hope that looked rather likely to be crushed as soon as the small talk was abandoned after choosing their meals from the menu at the small French restaurant Toni had chosen.

'You have a wonderful family, Pippa.' Toni smiled. 'You are very lucky.'

The undertone of sadness was unmistakable

and any hope Pip might have had of avoiding painful subjects went out the window. She wanted to know what had caused that sadness and—more dangerously—was more than willing to share her own.

And all it took to start the ball rolling was a single, tentative query.

'You weren't so lucky, Toni?'

His headshake was poignant. 'I've never told anyone about my upbringing. I was startled to find myself confessing that my mother had abandoned me to the less than willing care of my *nonna* when I first met you.' Toni toyed with the stem of the wineglass in front of him. Candlelight caught the ruby glints of his chosen wine but Pip was more transfixed by the sight of his fingers—straight out of that brief fantasy she'd had driving home the other night, only far more effective because they were *real*. And moving. One tapped the stem, as though Toni was undecided, or puzzled, about something.

'It wasn't as though I was aware of your own circumstances at the time,' he added. 'Of anything we might have had in common.'

'I'm sorry I didn't make it clear.' Pip kept her gaze on the play of light on the crystal glass. And on how still Toni's fingers now were as he listened carefully. 'I guess I prefer not to be judged on my past by people who don't know me.' She glanced up, her tone becoming a little defensive. 'And I didn't *abandon* my daughter.'

'I know that.' Toni's gaze held hers. 'And that is partly why you impress me so much.'

Pip felt a small glow of pleasure at those words. She impressed him? A *lot*?

'It's very obvious how much love there is in your home,' Toni continued. 'You—and your family—have made a success out of what could have been a disaster. What *was* a disaster in my own case because there was none of that kind of love.'

How amazing to find a reaction that engendered pride in what had shaped Pip's life to such an extent. The shame that James had magnified so destructively could, finally, be vanquished.

'It nearly was a disaster,' Pip admitted. 'It was my mother who kept everything together.'

'Tell me about it,' Toni invited. He touched Pip's hand when she hesitated briefly. 'Please.'

The plea in his touch as well as his tone was all the encouragement Pip needed.

'My father was a doctor,' she told Toni. 'A general practitioner. He was a wonderful man and I grew up wanting to be just like him—and to be a doctor who cared so much and was loved by his patients as much as he was.' Pip paused to mirror Toni's action and take a sip of her own wine. 'One day, when I was fifteen, he went out to mow the lawns and had a massive heart attack.'

The food arrived at that point and there was at least a minute of subdued silence. The waiter looked anxious.

'Is everything all right with your meals, sir?'

'It looks wonderful,' Toni assured him, but he didn't pick up any cutlery even after the waiter had gone. He was watching Pip.

'He died?' he asked quietly.

'Instantly.' Pip could smell the truffles and chicken on her plate. She picked up her fork but couldn't start eating. She put it down again. 'I saw it happen from my bedroom window. Mum called an ambulance and they tried their best but it was too late.' Pip tried to smile and lighten the atmosphere a fraction. 'It was so sudden! The engine on the lawnmower was still running when it was all over. Nobody had thought to turn it off.'

Toni seemed to have forgotten his dinner. 'What a dreadful thing to have happened. Especially when you were so young!' Toni's face was such a picture of sympathy, Pip could almost imagine the shine of tears in his eyes. 'Girls need their fathers, especially when they're in their teens.'

'It *was* awful. Mum and I were both devastated. Even now I try to avoid thinking about what it was like for the first few months.' Pip shook her head as though to clear the memory and a wisp of hair escaped her loose French plait. 'Anyway.' She tucked the strand of hair behind her ear. 'Please, eat, Toni. I'd hate this lovely food to get cold.'

For a minute they both tasted their food but Pip's unfinished story hung between them. What Toni really wanted to know about was Alice, wasn't it? When the waiter walked past their table moments later, with a nod of approval at the fact they were now eating, it gave her the opportunity to start talking again.

'I was so unhappy,' Pip said slowly. It was easy to look back and realise how badly she had behaved but it was much harder to admit it— especially to someone she would prefer to impress. 'And I was a self-centred teenager. I needed support and attention and I couldn't see that Mum needed it as much as I did. I set about trying to get what I wanted in totally the wrong way which only made everything worse, of course.'

Toni was nodding. It was more than nonjudgmental. 'I understand,' he said with a wry smile. 'I tried that myself for a while.'

'Did you ignore your schoolwork?'

'Only until I realised that using my mind was actually the only way I could control my own life.'

'Did you hang out with bad friends?'

'As much as it was possible in the kind of boarding schools I was sent to.' Toni's smile was broader. 'It was probably just as well I didn't have much freedom.' His face stilled then, ready to listen and accept whatever Pip wanted to tell him. 'You had more freedom?' he prompted.

Pip nodded sadly. 'Too much. I chose a new

group of friends simply because I knew my mother would not approve of them.' She took a half-hearted mouthful of food but then put her fork down again. 'One in particular, Catherine, was bad news but she had the reputation of being "cool". We got into trouble at school and she got me into parties with her older brother's friends from uni. There was a lot of alcohol and I discovered it could make me forget for a while.'

'How unhappy you were?'

Toni also seemed to have forgotten his food. He reached out and touched her. Just a stroke of a finger on the back of her hand, but it conveyed so much that it almost brought tears to Pip's eyes. He knew what was coming in this story and he understood. He accepted it. Pip had only told this tale to one other man and Toni's gesture couldn't be more different to the disgust she had seen in James's face. It gave her courage.

'Not just my unhappiness. I could stop feeling guilty about hurting my mother by how badly I was behaving. It was at the last one of those parties I went to that I let things get completely out of hand. Realising what I'd done was a wake-up call and I started to get my act together, but I'd left it just a bit too late.'

'You were pregnant?'

Pip nodded. 'I didn't figure it out for a while and then I was too terrified to tell anyone. I realised how much harder I'd made things for Mum and I was way too scared to make it worse by telling her I was pregnant. By the time I did, it was too late to even consider any option other than having the baby, and Mum was just as horrified as I knew she'd be.'

'She was angry?'

'The anger would have been easy to handle. I deserved it. What really got to me was how sad she was. She thought I had ruined my life. The father couldn't be traced easily. He'd only been in town on holiday from Australia and when Mum finally caught up with him he denied everything and refused any responsibility. We were on our own.'

'But you coped.' It was a statement rather than a question and Pip could hear the undertone of approval. Respect, even. Not that she could take the credit.

'Thanks to Mum. She refused to let me ruin

my chances of having a career. She made me finish school and then persuaded me to follow my dream of medical school. She said it's what Dad would have wanted for me as well, and if she didn't do anything more with the rest of her life than making that possible, she would be as happy as she could ever be again.'

They finished what they wanted of their meals in a rather thoughtful silence. It wasn't until the waiter appeared to collect their plates that Toni nodded.

'She's a strong woman, your mother,' he said approvingly. 'But she does seem…less than well at the moment.'

'I know. She's finally been to see our family doctor and he's referred her back to the surgeon who looked after her when she had the problem with gallstones.'

'That's good. I'm sure she will be fine.'

'Mmm.' Pip was happy to agree. 'I'm not going to let her do so much for me any more, though. It's funny, but it's only recently that I've realised how much more of a mother to Alice she is than I am.'

'And you don't like that?'

'I suppose I was flattered that Alice wanted to start calling me by my given name. To pretend we were sisters.'

'From my experience with working with families, I think that a lot of people aspire to being a friend to their children. It just needs to be balanced with the guidance a parent needs to provide.'

'And I've let Mum do most of the hard bits. She shouldn't have to do that twice in a lifetime.'

'But she loves it?'

'Yes. I can't just push her aside.'

Toni nodded. 'And you need to be able to do the job you're so good at.' Then he smiled. 'But you still need a life of your own outside working hours. What sort of things do you like to do for yourself, Pippa?'

He raised his eyebrows at the silence.

'Have you ever put what you wanted or needed just for yourself above the duty to your family or your studies?'

I tried that once, Pip thought. When she had believed she'd had a future with James. And that had been a disaster, hadn't it?

Toni nodded again at what he apparently read from her expression. 'I thought not,' he murmured. 'Maybe now is the time. You enjoyed eating out?'

'Oh, yes. But I'm afraid I spoilt it for you, talking about *my*self too much.'

His smile was nothing less than gorgeous. 'So, we'll redress the balance. Next time, I shall talk entirely about myself.'

Pip smiled back, unable to put a lid on the joy the words 'next time' had sparked.

'Do you like to dance? Go for walks in a forest or on a beach? Watch a movie?'

Pip's smile broadened. 'All of the above.'

Toni inclined his head in a satisfied nod. 'Then that's what we shall do,' he announced. 'All of the above.'

If he hadn't been so distracted by catching a glimpse of Pippa at the end of the corridor, Toni wouldn't have bumped into the edge of the meal trolley and found himself in the undignified position of having to collect the papers that had spilled from the folder he was carrying.

This was more than embarrassing. Toni Costa

had never let a woman get under his skin to this extent since the heartbreak of Ellen walking out on him. To creep, unbidden, into his thoughts almost constantly. To have his heart pick up speed and his awareness of his immediate surroundings fade at the mere sight of her at some distance.

It was disturbing.

Then again, when Pip stopped to help him, it no longer seemed to matter that her significance in his life was increasing exponentially. Or that there were others to witness the effects of his clumsiness. It was simply too good to be this close to her. To smell her perfume. To feel the brush of her hand as she passed him the pink 12-lead ECG trace.

'They're a traffic hazard, those meal trolleys, aren't they?'

Dio! Her smile was gorgeous. Toni wanted to kiss those curving lips and never mind who was watching. He'd wanted to kiss her last week when they'd been to dinner for a second time and even more last night when they had been to the movies. Why had it seemed so important to restrain himself? To decide that, for the first time in his life, he wasn't going to rush things. To let physical passion—or worse—the possibility of falling in love undermine rational thinking. He knew only too well how that could lead to disaster.

But it was *so* hard! Toni stood up so that he wasn't on the same level as those eyes but Pip's attention, fortunately, had been caught by a sheet of paper. She was still staring at it as she straightened and unconsciously followed his move to step to one side of the corridor and stop disrupting traffic.

'Good grief! This doesn't look very healthy.'

'No.' He may not be able to kiss her but Toni couldn't resist the opportunity to talk and keep Pippa close for just a little longer. 'Do you know what it is?'

'Supraventricular tachycardia?'

'How do you know it's not ventricular?'

'The QRS complexes are too narrow for that.' Pip was touching the paper as she counted. 'And it's fast enough to be a pretty impressive tachycardia. The rate must be over two hundred beats per minute.'

'Two hundred and thirty.'

'There's ST depression but it's probably rate-related. I wouldn't think a patient of yours would be suffering angina. If it *is* a patient of yours?' Raised eyebrows and the expression of such keen interest made Toni smile. Or was it the pleasure of an excuse to admire those curious gold flecks in the most beautiful eyes he'd ever seen?

'It's a trace from a twelve-year-old I've got in the ward. Unsuccessfully trialled on anti-epileptic medication by his GP.'

'For blackouts? Or was he having hypoxic seizures?'

Pippa's intelligence was just as sexy as every-thing else about this woman, Toni decided as he nodded. 'It's quite a common mistake, especially in this age group. What is that saying? About hoofbeats?'

'When you hear hoofbeats, think of horses, not zebras?'

'Yes. Only, in this instance, it is a zebra. You'd expect a convulsion in a child to be a disruption of the brain's electrical signals, not a lack of oxygen because the heart is not functioning properly.'

'Will he need a pacemaker?'

'I'm just on my way to discuss that with a cardiologist and refer him. Then I'll speak to the parents and preferably the boy as well.'

'He's young to have to face something as serious as this. Only Alice's age.'

'I don't like being anything less than honest with my patients. Often they cope better than their parents.'

'I'd better not keep you.' Pip looked pleasingly reluctant. 'But I'd better head back to the salt mine of Emergency. My lunch-break seems to be vanishing way too fast.'

'I'd better not keep you either, then.'

'No.' But Pip was smiling and neither of them moved.

The days were disappearing way too fast for Toni at present, thanks to their busy and often clashing workloads. They'd managed only three dates in the last two weeks.

'I enjoyed the movie last night.' It wasn't hard to sound sincere but the enjoyment had come more from holding Pippa's hand than anything he'd seen on the screen. He could almost still feel the delicate length of her fingers and the smoothness of her palm.

'So did I.'

'You cried.'

'It was a sad movie.' Pip grinned. 'And I saw you wiping your eyes so don't try to deny it!'

'Hey, I'm Italian—what do you expect?' Toni allowed himself to relax into the pleasure of Pip's company for just a second longer. It couldn't last, of course, as they were both expected elsewhere. 'Are you busy tonight?'

Pip grimaced. 'I'm on till 11 p.m.'

'Tomorrow night? Ah, no!' It was Toni's turn to look frustrated. 'I'm on call. Friday?'

Was it wishful thinking that made Pippa's face light up with pleasure?

'Yes, I'm free on Friday night.'

'Well, we've done the eating out and the movies. I think it's time to go dancing.'

It had to be the most sensual activity Pip had ever experienced.

They were both fully clothed and in public but the touch of Toni's hands and body couldn't have been more arousing.

Or more frustrating.

Pip had to exert enormous self-control not to simply drape herself over the man she was dancing with, close her eyes and think of nothing but the feel of him. She didn't dare raise her face to look at Toni in case he guessed what she was thinking.

What if he didn't share this level of attraction?

He hadn't made any attempt to kiss her yet, so maybe he didn't.

The chill that ran down Pip's spine at the thought made her realise just how close she was to falling in love with Toni...if it wasn't already too late. Memories of the agony in the wake of the failed relationship with James sounded a warning, but Toni already knew about Alice, didn't he? He liked her.

And Alice thought Toni was 'hot,' although she had been disappointed at news of the relationship's progress at breakfast-time today. Pip let herself twirl to the music and used the memory of the conversation to try and distract herself from the unnerving level of desire the activity was generating.

Shona had smiled at the news that Pip was going

out for an evening of dancing. 'I think you're being swept off your feet—in more ways than one.'

'Hmm.' Pip had unsuccessfully tried to hide a smile. 'Maybe it's got something to do with that Italian passion. It *is* kind of irresistible.'

Alice's jaw had dropped and her eyes had been like saucers. 'Are you and Toni...you know... like, *doing* it?'

'*Alice!*' Shona had been shocked.

'That wasn't what I meant,' Pip had said reprovingly. 'You can be passionate in ways that aren't physical, Alice.'

'Like what?'

'About things. Values. Toni's passionate about what he does for a job, which is why he's so good at it. And he's passionate about the importance of families.'

'Why?'

'I think a lot of Italian people place more value on their families than other cultures.' But Pip understood where a lot of Toni's passion in that area came from by now. She couldn't imagine how hard it must have been, growing up feeling such a lack, but it said a lot about Toni's personality and strength that he had chosen to dedicate his medical career to the care of children.

'So you're not doing it, then.' Alice sounded bored.

'Mind your own business,' Shona scolded. 'It's time you got ready for school, in any case.'

She gave Pip a curious glance when Alice stomped from the room.

'It's good if you're not rushing things,' she said. 'If something's worth having, it's worth waiting for.'

Pip's response had simply been a noncommittal sigh. It was none of Shona's business either, and Pip wasn't about to confess her growing frustration to anyone. Imagine if her mother could read her thoughts right now, as Toni's hand slid to the small of her back and pulled her even closer.

'So…' His voice tickled her ear. 'What shall we do next, Pippa Murdoch?'

'Ah…' Oh, God! Had her thoughts been transparent in her body language, even though she had tried to dampen them? Pip shuddered to think what Toni might think of her if she told him exactly what she thought they should do next.

She could swear his smile was knowing as the music finished and he led her back to their table, but his tone was perfectly innocent.

'On our next date,' he added belatedly. 'Assuming you want one, of course?'

'Mmm.' Pip had to quell the disappointment of knowing this one was nearly over. 'Of course,' she echoed.

'What's left on our list?' Toni leaned forward so that, for one heart-stopping moment, Pip thought he was about to kiss her. Then he smiled. 'Ah…yes. The walk. Forest or beach?'

'Ah…a beach would be nice,' Pip said faintly.

'Then again—' the look Pip was receiving made her wonder if Toni shared her thought that a beach might not be private enough '—maybe you could come to my house. I could cook for you.'

There could be no mistaking the underlying invitation. Toni could do a lot more than cook for Pip. What he was really asking was whether she was ready to take their relationship to the next level.

Pip was more than ready.

'I'd love that,' she said.

So the invitation had been issued and accepted. Something new came into the atmosphere between them and Pip knew exactly what it was. Anticipation. The kind of anticipation that gave her a peculiar feeling deep in her abdomen, like a lift dropping far too quickly. Was it possible that the reality could be a disappointment?

Not if the kiss she received when Toni took her home that night was anything to go by.

As a first kiss went, it couldn't have been more perfect.

Toni had climbed from the driver's seat to open her door, as he always did, and he had taken her hand to help her from the low sports car. What had not become customary was the way he kept hold of her hand to keep gently pulling until she was in his arms. So close, it was inevitable that his head should dip and their lips graze.

And then he let go of her hand and cradled her head instead, renewing the contact and taking it deeper.

So deep that Pip felt herself drowning in that

kiss, her lips clinging to his as though they were the only solid object that could save her. Melting inside at the first silky touch of his tongue.

Wanting more.

So much more.

The invitation had not only been issued and accepted. The agenda for the evening had just been clarified.

'You cooked pasta?'

Toni's shrug was eloquent. 'Hey, I'm Italian— what did you expect?'

'I had no expectations,' Pip responded. Which was perfectly true in regard to food at any rate. 'It looks delicious.'

'An old family recipe. Let me get you a glass of wine, Pippa.'

'Thank you.'

'Are you happy to stay in the kitchen? I may need to stir things occasionally.'

Pip sat down on an old spindle-backed wooden chair. 'I love kitchens,' she said warmly. 'They're the heart of a house.'

'They *are*!' Toni's smile gave Pip a very pleasurable glow at having said exactly the right thing. 'A place for family and food. What more could anyone need?'

Pip wasn't going to answer that one. She had been waiting days for this evening. Days in which the impossible had happened and the level of anticipation had heightened until Pip was as nervous as she had ever been on any date. 'This kitchen is gorgeous,' she said hurriedly, looking around at the old furniture with its polished wooden legs on a slate floor. At the row of gleaming copper pans hanging in front of an old, coal range. 'Your house is gorgeous.'

'Not what you expected?'

'No.' Pip had parked in front of the stately old home in a well-established suburb with some trepidation. 'I had imagined you in a townhouse, for some reason. All modern and sleek and low maintenance.' Not in a house with a huge garden that was crying out for a whole family.

'I love old things.' Toni was pouring two glasses of red wine. 'Traditions. I'm not sure of the word I need. Solidarity, perhaps? Things that have stood the test of time. That you can depend on.'

'Trustworthy?'

'Yes.' Toni handed Pip her glass and their hands touched. Pip's glance flicked up just as he ran his tongue over his lower lip. 'Are you trustworthy, Pippa Murdoch?'

The question seemed important enough to give Pip a frisson of something she couldn't identify. Or maybe it had been the glimpse of the tip of Toni's tongue that had undone her completely. Strangely, it had vanquished her nerves but her voice still sounded a little wobbly.

'Completely,' she said.

'I thought you might be.' Toni bent his head and kissed her. A lingering kiss that promised much more than it had time to deliver. Then he smiled at her. 'Are you hungry?'

Pip had never felt less like eating but Toni seemed to accept her vaguely strangled assent and turned back to the stovetop.

'How is Alice?'

'She's fine. Gone to a sleepover birthday party she was very excited about being invited to. Apparently Dayna is one of the "cool" girls at school.'

'Like your friend Catherine was?'

'Lord, I hope not!' But Pip smiled. Fancy Toni remembering a detail like that from a conversation that was now weeks old. He really did listen, didn't he? As though whatever she said was important to him. She liked that. Very much.

'And your mother?'

'She's OK. I think she's lost a bit of weight recently. I'm watching her colour carefully, too, because I thought I caught a hint of jaundice, but she hasn't mentioned any abdominal pain. She's gone out tonight, too, with a friend. To a movie, I think.'

'Not a sleepover?'

'No.' Pip laughed as she watched Toni grinding black pepper over the saucepan. He swapped the grinder for the bottle of red wine, sloshed a good measure into the sauce and then moved to top up Pip's glass.

Maybe it was the mention of sleepover parties that had increased the electricity in the air—reminding them both of that unspoken agenda. Or maybe it was the combination of red wine and the rich aroma of a creamy pasta sauce. Pip found herself holding her breath as she watched Toni slowly put the bottle down on the table. With his hand free, he touched the loose waves of Pip's hair, lifting the weight from her shoulder and letting it drift through his fingers.

'Beautiful,' he said softly. 'It catches the light.' He lifted another handful but this time he didn't let it spill. Instead, he held it clear as he reached down to kiss the side of her neck. '*You* are beautiful,' he murmured.

Any hope of being able to eat a single mouthful of the food Toni was preparing evaporated. Somehow Pip found her arms around Toni's neck, being lifted to her feet, a trail of kisses leading from her neck to her lips.

It was several minutes before she could take in enough air or the inclination to speak.

'I think,' she whispered then, 'that you should turn that stove off for a while.'

The sauce did not get reheated that night.

Hours later, when Pip returned to the kitchen to collect her car keys, the sight of the abandoned meal reminded her she hadn't eaten. She was not remotely hungry, however. How could she be when she had never in her life felt this kind of satisfied glow?

The knowledge that every conceivable desire she might have had just been so completely fulfilled.

Toni had surpassed every fantasy of what he would be like as a lover. His kisses…his touch…his ability to take control and yet to be so astonishingly gentle at the same time had been a revelation.

It had only been with the greatest reluctance that Pip had finally extracted herself from the bed with the antique brass bedhead.

'Stay, *cara*.'

'I can't. Not tonight. I'm expected home and it's too late to ring.'

'Your mother won't approve?'

'It's not that.' Pip fastened the catches of her bra that felt curiously too small. The lacy fabric grazed oversensitised nipples and made it impossible not to remember exactly what it was like to feel the caress of Toni's lips and tongue. Even his teeth. 'Next time, I'll stay,' Pip promised. She picked up her jeans. 'That is, if you invite me again.'

Her wrist was grasped so fast Pip gasped. Then she let out a small shriek as the ensuing tug had her tumbling back amongst the rumpled bed-clothes. Against the smooth skin of Toni's chest where she could feel his warmth and smell the sheer maleness of his body.

'How could you possibly think you wouldn't be, after *that*?'

'Oh, I don't know,' Pip murmured mischievously. 'Maybe it wasn't so good for you.'

'Then you weren't listening to a word I said,' Toni growled.

Pip grinned. 'You were talking in Italian.' And how sexy had *that* been? Pip hadn't needed any expertise in another language to guess the meaning of those phrases, but Toni wasn't to know that.

'Then next time,' he announced, 'I will speak in English.'

'No.' Pip returned a final, lingering kiss. 'I

don't want anything to be different. It was just perfect the way it was.'

The echo of those lyrical phrases was still with Pip as she let herself quietly into her house. She could have stayed with Toni. She supposed. Shona would have understood. But what if Alice had become ill during the night and she had been absent? Selfishly ensconced with a lover? The idea of being in a relationship intense enough to include overnight visits needed a bit of time to get used to. For all of them, she suspected.

Was that why Shona was still up? Pip hadn't expected to see the kitchen light still on. Or to hear her mother call.

'Pip? Is that you?'

'Yes, I'm home. Are you all right, Mum?'

The silence made her frown. Pip dismissed her plan of going straight to bed where she would have used the darkness to relive every moment of the last few hours and keep that satisfied glow alive. Instead, she moved towards the kitchen.

'Mum?'

Shona was sitting at one end of the table. She looked as though she had been crying.

'Can you sit down for a bit, Pip? I need to talk to you.'

CHAPTER FIVE

THE sensation of fulfilment vanished utterly.

'What's wrong?' Pip asked sharply. 'Has something happened to Alice?'

Shona shook her head. To Pip's horror, a tear escaped and rolled slowly down her mother's cheek.

'You're not upset that I've been out with Toni, are you?'

Shona smiled through her tears. 'Oh, no! How could I be? This is the best thing that could have happened. For all of us. Especially now.'

There was an undertone to Shona's words that Pip didn't like. She sat down on the chair closest to her mother.

'I don't understand, Mum. What's upset you so much?'

The brightness in Shona's voice was forced

and made her words sound anything but casual. 'I had an appointment today. At the hospital.'

'What? Why didn't you tell me?'

'I did tell you that I was being sent to see the surgeon again.'

'You didn't say *when*. I would have come with you.'

'I know. I didn't want you to, love. And, anyway, that was a couple of weeks ago. I've had lots of other tests since then.'

A sense of foreboding took hold of Pip. 'But why didn't you *say* something?'

'I didn't have all the information. And you're so happy at the moment. I didn't want to spoil things.'

Foreboding became dread.

'Tell me,' Pip said slowly, 'what the surgeon said.'

Shona wiped away the last traces of her tears as she took a noticeably deeper breath. 'They found something on the ultrasound and I got referred to another doctor. In oncology. I had an MRI scan today.'

'Oh, my God!' This was unbelievable. Pip had floated through her day at work, in excited anticipation of what she had known would happen between herself and Toni tonight, totally oblivious to something major happening in her own family. How selfish was that? 'And?' she prompted her mother.

'And I have cancer,' Shona said calmly. 'Of my pancreas.'

The bottom was falling out of Pip's world. She could hear an odd buzzing in her head and she felt faintly nauseated. She could never have anticipated being blindsided like this. To find her mother had exactly what she had feared most when she'd taken Alice to that first appointment with Toni. The fear had been dismissed. It *couldn't* be happening again—to Shona instead of Alice.

'It's at something they call Stage llA. I'm not sure exactly what it means, although they did tell me. It went over my head a bit. Apparently it's past the stage where I could expect any kind of cure, though.'

'No!' The word was torn from Pip. Fear had replaced dread. Mixed with it was a very uncomfortable level of guilt. She closed her eyes. 'You've

known about it for most of the day and you didn't tell me. You let me go out on a…a *date*!'

'I needed a bit of time to get my own head around this,' Shona responded. 'And I had to wait until Alice was out. I don't want her to know.'

'She'll have to know.'

'Not yet,' Shona said urgently. 'Promise me, Pip—you won't tell her until *I'm* ready.'

Pip's silence was taken as acquiescence, which was hardly surprising if her expression reflected what she was thinking. She would have promised Shona anything right then, if it could have made a blind bit of difference to the outcome.

'Things are changing,' Shona continued thoughtfully. 'And I really don't want to spoil them.'

She had said that earlier. She had allowed Pip to be selfish enough to revel in the start of a promising romance and, by doing so, she had taken away Pip's right to choose. As though she was still a child who needed important decisions made *for* her. Unexpectedly, resentment bloomed amongst a maelstrom of even darker emotions.

'I can't believe you didn't tell me. That you've been dealing with this for weeks by yourself. That you let me go out tonight of all nights, when I should have been here. With you.'

'That's precisely why.' Shona patted Pip's hand. 'You would have stayed if you'd known and I had the feeling tonight was going to be special with it being the first time you've been to Toni's house.'

Pip might have been embarrassed if she'd focused on how accurately her mother had interpreted the significance of tonight's date. Or if she had given a second's thought to what had happened over the last few hours. Funny how something that had seemed so incredibly special had suddenly become insignificant. Something she could even feel ashamed of.

'You wouldn't have gone if you'd known, would you?' Shona prompted.

'Of course I wouldn't.'

'And that would have changed things. It might have been enough to stop them completely.'

Would it? Toni would have understood if she had cancelled the date due to a family emergency.

He would have approved of where her loyalties lay. But what about the weeks or months ahead? Would the start of any physical relationship have been given any priority in what was likely to be a time of intense family commitment?

Probably not. But because they had become so close tonight, it would be far more difficult to shut Toni from her life than it would have been if she'd stayed home and had this conversation with her mother so much earlier. Not telling her—keeping even a hint of the news away from her—had been an unselfish act on Shona's part. While Pip could feel resentful at having had her free choice removed, she could understand the motivation. The love it was based on.

'You're far more important than anything else I have going on in my life, Mum. *This* is far more important. I'm going to help you fight this.'

Shona smiled sadly. 'Don't think I don't want to fight it, love, and I will…but we need to be realistic.'

'I'll go and talk to your doctors tomorrow. Find out exactly what we're dealing with. I can't believe you went to this appointment today by yourself.'

'I wasn't really expecting to find out what I did.'

'Did they mention treatment options?'

'They told me so much that most of it went over my head. I can't remember a lot.'

'Which is why I should have been with you.'

'I asked for another appointment on Monday. So that you could come and hear everything and then help me decide on what's going to best.'

'Did they say anything about the possibility of surgery?'

'Yes. They talked about surgery and radiotherapy and chemotherapy and even clinical trials I might like to consider. What I did understand was that anything done might buy me a little more time or make me more comfortable but it's not going to change the outcome. I may only have a few months.'

Pip couldn't hold back her tears now. Or the fear. Or the feeling that she was a child again—no older than Alice. The comfort of being held in her mother's arms was indescribable. And *so* poignant. It was some time before either woman could control their grief.

'If I need surgery,' Shona said eventually, 'I'm

going to tell Alice it's the same as the gallstone operation I had.'

'Why?'

'I don't want her to make a connection between what's wrong with me and what's wrong with her. It would be scary.'

'Alice doesn't have cancer.'

'No, but she has an abnormality in her pancreas. It could be that there's a genetic link, couldn't there? That she might be more at risk herself?'

'I don't know,' Pip admitted. 'But I do know that Alice is going to be fine. It's you we need to concentrate on at the moment.'

'I do want more time.'

'Of course you do. *I* want more time for you as well. As much as possible.'

'I don't need too much. Just enough to see if Toni is the one for you. Whether you can make a family together when...when I'm not here.' Shona stroked Pip's hair. 'That's all I need to know, Pip. That you and Alice are both going to be safe...and happy.' She gripped her daughter's hand. 'He's a wonderful man, darling. Alice thinks so, too, although I think the words she used were "hot" and "cool"—which don't seem to be contradictory for teens these days.'

They both smiled.

'He seems totally smitten with you,' Shona added, 'and I've never seen you as happy as you've been in the last month. Don't let this change things, Pip. Please!'

How could it *not* change things?

The first, and possibly most unexpected, change occurred well before the appointment Pip was dreading on Monday when the official confirmation of her mother's prognosis would come.

If she had given any thought to Toni during the sleepless hours of that first night, it had been poignant. Their relationship was so newborn and fragile and there could be no room in her life for romance now. Not when her emotional energy had to be focused on the needs of her mother and her daughter.

The time she had spent with Toni that evening had been too good to be true. Magic but selfish. A gift her mother had wanted her to have, but in some ways it might have been easier if Pip hadn't experienced what Toni had to offer as a lover. She wasn't going to be desirable as a romantic companion for the foreseeable future, and it was too much to hope that Toni cared about her enough already to take this in his stride.

He wouldn't drop her immediately, of course, he was far too nice for that, but the baggage she brought with her had suddenly become much heavier, almost too heavy to lift, and it would have to start making a difference. It would become too much and their relationship could falter and die, inch by inch.

Maybe it would be better to let him escape now before things became miserable.

But Toni had other ideas.

The fact that he could tell something was wrong simply by the way she said hello when he rang the next day was a surprise. The depth of concern in his query about what was wrong that went unanswered was almost enough to reduce Pip to tears and the way he took control was irresistible.

'Be at your gate in five minutes,' he ordered.

'I am coming to take you for a drive and you will tell me what is upsetting you, *bella*.'

Shona had waved her off. 'Be as long as you like, love,' she instructed. 'Alice and I need time to argue about what take-aways we want to order and what we're going to watch on television tonight.'

Normal Saturday night family stuff when normality was no longer a real option. Pip waited at her gate with confusion thrown into the maelstrom of her heightened emotions.

Sliding into Toni's car and accepting his kiss could have been an exciting new normality after last night, but Pip had to pull away. At least, she tried to, but Toni held her—his fingers gripping her shoulders with determination.

'Whatever is wrong? Is my kissing so bad?'

Pip tried to laugh. Instead, she burst into tears.

'Drive…' she managed to choke out. 'Please… I don't want Alice to see me crying.'

Toni drove the shortest distance. Just around the corner until they were out of sight of her house. He pulled the car to a jerky stop, snapped open both his own and Pip's safety belts and then pulled her into his arms.

For the longest time, he said nothing.

Demanded no explanations.

He simply held her and let her cry, and if Pip hadn't realised she was in love with this man before, she could have no doubt about it now. He had no idea what she was so upset about but he was still prepared to hold and comfort her. It was like the way he accepted Alice as part of her life. Whoever she was and whatever baggage she brought with her was made to feel acceptable.

And when she was finally ready to talk, he listened with the same kind of attentiveness with which he had heard the story of her past. He held her as she spoke and every subtle movement of his body and hands implied willingness to be there. To support her.

'And she waited to tell you this because she knew it was our…first time together?'

'Yes.'

'She is a wise woman.'

'You think so?' Pip couldn't help the seed of new hope being sown. A hope that this wouldn't be enough to drive Toni from her life.

'I know so. She knew that you would have shut yourself away from me if you'd known. You care too much for the people you love to allow something as selfish as a lover at such a time.' Toni kissed Pip's hair gently. 'But you cannot do that now, can you, *cara*?'

'No.' There was no way in the world Pip could voluntarily give up what Toni was giving her.

'I can help. I can give you strength.'

'It's not very romantic.' Pip felt obliged to at least issue a warning. 'I won't be able to swan off for things like dinners and dancing and walks on the beach for a while.'

'Romance can come in many forms,' Toni said seriously. 'Maybe this will be the most important one.'

'It's a lot to ask of you.'

'It's what friends are for.' Toni kissed her hair again. 'And we are more than friends, aren't we?'

'Yes.' Pip turned her face and received another kiss, this time on her lips. It was a kiss that carried all the strength of passion and yet there was nothing overtly sexual about it. It was like nothing Pip had ever experienced. More than sex. More than friendship. It conveyed hope. The possibility that Toni had fallen in love with her to the same degree she had with him. It was enough to cause the sting of tears again. Was that what reminded Toni of why she was sitting in his car?

'And you have an appointment to go to with your mother on Monday?'

'Yes. She was, understandably, a bit hazy on the medical details and options for treatment. I want to make sure we have all the information we need so I can help her decide the best next step.'

'Would you like me to be there as well?'

'That's sweet of you, but, no, I think it would be better if it was just me and Mum.'

'You'll come and talk to me afterwards?'

'Of course.'

'I will be at home on Monday evening. I will be waiting for you.'

'Stage llA is where the tumour extends beyond the pancreas but there's no involvement of the celiac axis or the superior mesenteric artery.' The oncologist showed Pip the pictures from the MRI scan. 'No regional lymph node metastasis and no distant metastasis.'

Which sounded as though things could have been a lot worse, but Pip had done some research of her own over the weekend and was all too aware of how difficult it was to control this type of cancer. And how fast it could progress if you were one of the unluckier victims.

'I need you to go over the treatment options again,' Shona said. 'So that Pip can help me choose what to do.'

'As we discussed, there's surgery. It's the only form of therapy with any potential for cure and even with a tumour like yours, situated in the head of the pancreas, we could expect good results. Palliation of symptoms at the least and a life expectancy greater than the average for inoperable pancreatic cancer.'

'Which is?' Pip asked tightly.

'Approximately ten months.'

'What about follow-up treatment?'

The surgeon nodded. 'Of course. We'll look at

radiation and/or chemotherapy and we'll treat anything else as it crops up.'

Like pain, Pip thought miserably. 'What's involved with the surgery?'

'It's a pancreaticduodenectomy.'

'Goodness!' Shona actually smiled. 'It must take as long to say that as do the surgery.'

But it was no laughing matter. 'We remove the head of the pancreas,' the surgeon continued soberly. 'And the adjacent duodenum plus the lower bile duct and a portion of the stomach. This will take out the tumour and the adjacent lymph nodes.'

'That's major,' Pip murmured.

'But with very good statistics as far as mortality and morbidity are concerned.'

'How will I eat?' Shona sounded stunned. 'How much of my stomach gets taken out?'

'About half. You'll be able to eat normally though not in large quantities. Your diet may need some adjustment but the dieticians will help you with that. It can be more difficult to digest food so you may need replacement pancreatic enzymes or hormones after the surgery.

You may also develop diabetes and need to take insulin.'

'How soon could you schedule the surgery?' Pip asked.

'As early as next week if that's the route you want to take.'

'I'm not sure about that,' Shona said. 'I need to think about it. How long would I have to be in hospital for?'

'At least a week.'

'And it would mean weeks of recuperation on top of that, wouldn't it? As long as it took after I had my gallbladder out?'

'Maybe longer, if you're starting other treatments in that period.'

'So that might represent a significant percentage of the time I have left. I'm not sure I want to spend it in and out of hospital.'

The short silence underlined the fact that there would be no escape from hospital and medical intervention in the near future if Shona wanted to put up any kind of fight against what was happening.

She sighed deeply. A resigned sound. 'Well,

that's going to need careful planning,' she said heavily. 'We've got the care of a house and a young child to take into account.'

'We'll manage,' Pip said, yet again, that evening. 'I'll take care of everything, Mum. I'll juggle my shifts so I can drop Alice off at school. She can come to the hospital after school and wait for me. Or she's old enough to come home by herself and be alone for a while.'

'Why am I going to be alone?' Alice breezed into the kitchen, heading straight past the table towards the pantry. 'Have we got any chocolate biscuits, Nona?'

'You've just had your dinner.'

'Yeah, but I'm still hungry.' They could hear packages being rustled in the depths of the large cupboard. 'So why am I going to be by myself?'

'I might need to go into hospital for a few days,' Shona said casually. 'For an operation.'

'Oh…' Alice shut the cupboard, having extracted a new packet of biscuits. 'Like last time?'

'Yes.' Shona gave Pip a warning glance. 'Just like last time.'

'Do I have to go and stay with that friend of yours? The one with the false teeth?' Alice gave a visible shudder. 'It was gross!'

'No,' Pip said. 'I'm going to look after you.'

Alice looked surprised and then pleased. 'Cool.' She ripped open the packet of biscuits. 'Can I go to the movies with Dayna tomorrow night?'

'No.' Pip couldn't believe how callous Alice was sounding. She opened her mouth to say something to that effect, but caught another look from her mother.

'Not on a school night,' Shona said evenly. 'Maybe at the weekend.'

Pip watched her daughter leave the kitchen, her mouth full of chocolate and wafer. Her eyebrows rose. 'Aren't you going to tell her to go easy on those biscuits?'

Shona shook her head. 'It doesn't matter. And don't be angry because she doesn't seem to care. She doesn't know the truth and that's the way I want it for the moment.'

'The fact that you even need to go to hospital should be enough to wake her up into thinking about someone other than herself.'

'She's a teenager.' Shona smiled. 'The job description is to think of no one but yourself, isn't it? Besides, we've been here before. She stayed with Mary of the false teeth for a few days and then everything was back to normal. No big deal.'

Except that nothing was going to be back to normal this time. Not ever.

'Are you sure you can cope?' Shona sounded worried now. 'On top of working? There's more than just supervising Alice and being a taxi. There's all the housework and cooking and shopping and washing and—'

'I'll manage,' Pip assured her. 'You'll see.'

Her mother nodded. 'I'm sure I will. I've never given you the space to try managing everything yourself, have I? Not the best way of parenting, but I guess I got used to feeling needed.'

'You'll always be needed, Mum. Just not as a housekeeper or babysitter.'

'It'll help to know you can manage without me.' Shona tried, but failed, to summon a smile. 'One less thing to worry about, anyway. And, Pip?'

'Yes?'

'You're to go and have at least one more date with that gorgeous boyfriend of yours before I go into hospital.'

The date was low key. A coffee and a talk in a kitchen that held no delicious aroma of a meal that would go uneaten because passion intervened.

'Surgery is definitely the best option,' Toni agreed, still holding Pip's hands after listening to her account of the interview. 'The only option.'

'It's going to be hard on Mum, having to go through the pain and recuperation period without knowing whether it'll make much difference to the outcome.'

'Far better than not going through it and thinking it *could* have made a difference.'

'I'm not going to be able to get out much. It's going to be difficult keeping the house going and looking after Alice and keeping up with work. I don't want to take time off before I really have to because it could mean waiting another year or more to get into the GP training scheme.'

'I can help,' Toni said decisively. 'We can take Alice out at weekends to let your mother rest. I can cook for you at your home.' His thumbs were stroking her palms. 'I can be here whenever you need to escape. To have someone to talk to. To hold you. Whatever you need, Pippa.'

The kind of things any good friend would offer at a time like this. Was it so wrong to want more?

'I need you.' Pip confessed. 'I think I would like you to hold me, Toni. Is that all right?'

Toni said something in Italian as he pushed back his chair and helped Pip to her feet. Into his arms. Whatever it was, the tone made her feel as though it was her giving something to him instead of so completely the other way round. He still made it feel like that when he took her to his bed a short time later.

Their love-making had a quality that could never have been there the first time. Could never have been there at all, if not for the sadness Pip was having to deal with. It was about far more than physical attraction or release. It was a confirmation of intent. A willingness to be there no matter what. To provide comfort.

Love, even? The kind of love that could endure and last a lifetime?

Maybe. But it didn't matter if it wasn't because right now Pip was living from moment to moment.

And this moment was perfect.

'You are supposed to come *straight* home after school. It's nearly six o'clock! Where the hell have you *been*?'

'At the mall. With Dayna.'

'Why weren't you answering your phone? I've been worried sick.'

'My phone's dead. I forgot to charge it last night.'

'That's not good enough, Alice. I've got more than enough to do right now, without having to worry about where you are.'

'Who said you had to worry? If I'm old enough to be home by myself, I'm old enough to go to the mall if I want to. It's only ten minutes' walk away. You can't stop me!'

'Don't bet on it!'

They were so alike, Toni thought as he watched Pip and Alice facing each other off across the kitchen table. Pip had probably been just as independent and determined when she had been Alice's age. He couldn't imagine Pip treating Shona with such disdain, however. Was it a generational thing or was it that the dynamic between this particular mother and daughter was flawed? Despite nearly two weeks of trying to establish new routines and roles, Pip was clearly still struggling to find her feet.

From Toni's perspective, it was easy to see where the problem lay. Due to circumstances entrenched over many years, Pip was firmly cast in the role of a big sister. Much closer to being a friend than a parent. A dynamic that worked brilliantly on some occasions, such as the hilarious afternoon last weekend when Toni had offered to give Alice her first driving lesson and Pip had supervised from the back seat of the car. Or the night at home when Alice had tried to teach both Pip and Toni the dance moves she had picked up from the new music video she had borrowed from Dayna.

At other times, though, like now, Pip had no idea where to put boundary lines. It suggested a total lack of confidence in her ability as a parent.

Of being prepared to risk popularity to provide the kind of control and guidance a child needed. And if she didn't take the plunge now, it wasn't going to get any easier as Alice headed into adolescence. The shadow of having to take on this role permanently had to be weighing heavily on Pip's mind, but Toni was holding back from making any promises of being there to help.

It was a privilege, being allowed inclusion in this family at such a time. A chance to show Pippa how deeply he cared but also a chance to make sure his trust in her was not misplaced. He couldn't afford to make a mistake. Not just for himself. Or for Pippa. Alice was important, too. It was a trial by fire for this romance but Toni wasn't put off. Not at all. In a curious way, he was enjoying the argument. The dynamics of being on the inside of a normal family-style dispute that could be heated but the underlying love was never lost. Just the kind of interaction that had been missing from his own life.

'Just don't do it again,' Pip was saying. 'In future, you let me know where you are and what time you'll be home.'

'OK.'

Toni wasn't surprised at how readily Alice agreed to such a minor restriction to her freedom. Text messages could easily be less than honest, couldn't they? He had the horrible feeling Pip was buying into a whole lot more trouble but it wasn't his place to intervene. As much as he would like to be more, he was still merely an observer. Moral support for Pip. Only included because it was what Pip wanted.

'That's cool.' Alice sounded placating now. 'What's for dinner?'

'Spaghetti Bolognese,' Toni told her.

Alice groaned. 'I think I'm turning into an Italian.'

'Don't knock it.' Pip's tone was short. 'It's only thanks to Toni that you're getting fed at all tonight.'

'Don't stress,' Alice commanded. 'How's Nona?'

'A little better. Are you going to come and visit her tonight?'

'Nah. I've got a heap of homework to do. She's always asleep when I come in anyway.'

'She still knows when you're there.'

'She's been in hospital for ages.'

'There were some complications after her operation. Now they need to work out the best diet for her when she gets home.'

'Oh.' The unspoken complaint that the visits and someone else being the centre of everybody's attention were becoming tedious hung in the air, and Toni found himself gritting his teeth.

Alice had no idea how sick her grandmother was and Toni was convinced it would be better for her to know the truth despite Pip's acquiescence to Shona's wish of keeping it from the child. He wasn't about to push the issue, however. Pip was dealing with more than enough, without him adding to her stress levels. She was looking even more pale and tired this evening and what Toni wanted to do was to take her in his arms and look after her—another argument was the last thing she needed. What if she really disagreed with him? Would she ask him to step aside and let her manage her own family in her own way? Toni wasn't ready to test those boundaries. He didn't want to step aside.

'When's she coming home?' Alice was looking at her phone—the half-smile suggesting she had received a welcome message.

'In a few days.'

'That's good.' But Alice's attention was now on the screen of her mobile phone as she responded to a text message. Did Pip not notice the blatant discrepancy of batteries that were no longer flat?

'You should get on with that homework. Dinner won't be for half an hour and if you get it done, you could come into the hospital with me later.'

Pip turned to Toni when Alice left the kitchen and he was only too willing to accept her kiss.

'Sorry,' she murmured.

'What for?'

'Having to listen to us scrapping. Just what you need after a long day at work.'

'You don't need it either.' Toni kissed her again. 'I wish I could make this easier for you.'

'You are. I wouldn't have coped so far without you. You're a rock.'

'I could do more.' He could talk to Alice. Maybe tell her a few home truths and explain the necessity for making her changed relationship with her mother more positive. It was quite possible she would appreciate the opportunity to make her own, real contribution to this family in a time of crisis.

'You don't need to,' Pip assured him. 'It'll be better when Mum's back at home. Things will settle down then.'

'Time of death.' Pip looked wearily at her watch. 'Three forty-five p.m.'

The frail body of their ninety-three-year-old patient was a silent testimony to failure. Pip had spent nearly two hours trying to hold back the inevitable after this elderly woman had come in with severe heart failure exacerbated by pneumonia. She gently closed the woman's eyes and then stripped off her gloves. 'Are any relatives here?'

'No.' Suzie was starting to pick up wrappers and discarded equipment. They had known they were probably fighting a losing battle when faced with heart failure bad enough to cause the bloodstained froth the woman had presented with around her mouth, but Pip had tried everything.

Oxygen, nitrates, morphine, diuretics. Continuous positive airway pressure via a face mask and a raft of other drugs to try and combat the ensuing cardiac rhythm abnormalities. They had gone through the protocol for the subsequent cardiac arrest but Pip had called it well before the time they might have spent on another patient. It had been clearly pointless but at least they all knew they had given it a shot.

'It was a neighbour who called the ambulance,' Suzie said. 'And there's no next of kin listed in her notes.'

No family to talk to, then. Nobody to mourn the loss of a mother or grandmother. There were still things Pip needed to do for this patient, however. Forms to fill in. Did she have enough information to complete a death certificate herself or would she need to refer the case to the coroner?

'I need to have a word to Brian before I do the death certificate,' she told Suzie. 'You OK to finish up in here?'

'Absolutely.' Suzie touched Pip's arm. 'Are *you* OK?'

'Sure. She was ninety-three after all and she'd been battling increasing heart failure for a while, by the look of her notes. I guess any death just comes a bit close to home at the moment.'

'How *is* your mother?'

'Picking up. She's able to get out of bed for part of the day now and I don't feel so bad leaving her when I'm at work.' Which wasn't quite true. Pip was carrying a sense of guilt with her on a permanent basis but she couldn't afford to interrupt her training programme for too long and Shona wasn't about to let her. How would she support Alice if she let herself slip too far back? 'She's got a good friend who comes every day to stay with her and she has been taking her to some of the radiotherapy appointments. I'll have to take leave if she deteriorates, though.'

Or should that have been 'when' not 'if', Shona deteriorated. With a last look at the patient on the bed in Resus 2, Pip moved to find her senior colleague to check on death-certificate requirements. It was hard to try and shake off the weight of sadness that still caught her out at times but it was hardly unexpected just now, having tried and then failed to prevent someone dying.

'The notes are pretty comprehensive,' Brian told her a short time later. 'And you got a chest X-ray done, which confirms the pneumonia. See if you can get hold of her GP, but I think the background we've got here and the length of time you were treating her in ED means there's no reason for you not to complete certificating the cause of death.' He gave Pip an intense glance. 'You look done in.'

'It hasn't been a great day,' Pip admitted. 'And this wasn't the best way to finish.'

The GP's receptionist promised to return the phone call as soon as the doctor was between patients. Pip stayed sitting beside the telephone at the central desk, filling in what she could on the forms.

Thank goodness her working day would soon be over. It hadn't been all that great even at its beginning, but whose fault had that been?

Staying up until the early hours, preparing a casserole for tonight's dinner so that all Shona needed to do was turn the oven on. Making a school lunch for Alice and ironing the horrible pleats into the skirt of her school uniform. It could all have been done at a much more reasonable hour if Pip hadn't spent the evening with Toni.

It had been the first time they had been alone together at his house in longer than she cared to count, and Pip wouldn't have gone if Shona and her friend, Mary, hadn't virtually pushed her out the door.

'We're going to play Scrabble,' Shona had said. 'And I intend to win.'

'I'll be here until you get home,' Mary had added. 'And I don't expect to see you this side of midnight. Shona's told me all about that gorgeous young man of yours.'

Alice had been on the computer, instant messaging her friends, and had seemed completely disinterested in the fact that Pip had been going out.

'Have fun,' had been all she'd said.

'Fun' wasn't exactly in Pip's vocabulary these days, but the time with Toni had been like a temporary release from prison. An escape into paradise.

And she hadn't felt guilty. Well, not much, anyway. Surely she owed Toni that little bit of time and undivided attention? He'd been amazing ever since the news of Shona's diagnosis. If she'd needed a test to see whether she'd found the man she wanted to spend the rest of her life with, she couldn't have devised a better one. A trial by fire, no less, that he was passing with flying colours.

Being overtired to start her working day had been a small price to pay for the reprieve last night had given her.

In response to the beeping and message on her pager, Pip lifted the telephone receiver to take the incoming call, fully expecting to find herself talking to her patient's GP.

But the name wasn't right.

'Bob Henley, did you say?'

'That's right. I'm the headmaster at Alice's school.'

Pip drew in a quick breath. 'Is she all right?'

'She's not unwell.' The headmaster cleared his throat. 'We do have a bit of a problem that we need to discuss, though, and I'd rather not do it on the phone. Would it be possible for you to come to the school?'

'Of course.' It was just another aspect of parenting she was going to have to get used to. What on earth had Alice done to get herself into trouble? 'When? I'm almost finished work for today. I could come almost immediately.'

'That might be best. I've got Alice here in my office at the moment. We'll both be waiting for you.'

CHAPTER SIX

ALICE was sitting, all alone, on a seat outside the headmaster's office.

Pip finally slowed her pace. 'What's going on, Alice?'

'Nothing.'

Which turned out to be precisely what the headmaster was concerned about.

'Alice just isn't doing anything at the moment,' he informed Pip. 'No work in class, no homework, no effort in any direction that we can detect. We're worried about her.'

'Oh.' Pip looked at Alice, who was now slumped in a chair beside her in front of Bob Henley's desk. She was staring at the floor and gave no indication that she was at all bothered by the fact she was in trouble.

Where had the child gone, who had rushed

home from school eager to share the day's accomplishments or bathe in the glow of parental pride engendered by a good end-of-term report?

Pip couldn't also help wondering where those pleats she had painstakingly pressed into Alice's school uniform last night had gone. Melted by the large splodge of green paint, perhaps? Her gaze travelled swiftly over her daughter as though seeing her from Bob's point of view. A lot of hair had escaped the ponytail, a thread dangled from a drooping hem on the stained uniform and socks that should have been knee-high were slumped around ankles. From head to toe, Alice looked scruffy. And supremely bored.

'We've had to confiscate her mobile phone and separate her from her friend, Dayna. Their behaviour in class has simply become too disruptive.'

'I had no idea,' Pip sighed.

'Of course not. We thought it would be helpful to bring you into the picture sooner rather than later.' Bob made a steeple of his fingers. 'This has been a rather dramatic change for Alice over the last couple of months. I wondered if you knew of anything going on outside school that could be making the difference.'

Pip sat up a little straighter. Had she been neglectful as a parent in not informing the school of Shona's illness? She hadn't even thought of doing so, thanks to Shona's insistence that things remain as normal as possible for Alice's sake.

To give her time to get used to changes.

Like the change her relationship with Toni was causing.

If the school had noticed a difference over a period of nearly two months, that meant the deterioration in Alice's behaviour coincided with Pip's relationship with Toni and predated any hidden tension she might have picked up since the diagnosis of Shona's illness. But it had been Alice who had encouraged Pip to find a boyfriend. Did she now resent the fact that Pip had someone else of significance in her life?

And if that resentment was enough to cause the negative change in attitude at school, how much worse would it be in a few months' time—or however long Shona might have left?

A clear flash of her own resentment towards her mother in initially withholding the truth about her condition swept through Pip. As well as another resentment that Toni had sparked by suggesting Shona was wrong in trying to protect Alice like this. That children had as much right to honesty as adults did. That they might find that trying to protect her would only make things a lot worse in the long term.

This seemed to be a clear warning that Toni was right.

'Things *are* a bit unsettled at home just now,' Pip told the headmaster. 'Alice's grandmother isn't well.'

'I'm sorry. Is it serious?'

Pip gave a single, brief nod. Bob Henley looked taken aback and his gaze flicked to Alice, but she was still staring at the floor and gave every impression of not listening to a word being said around her.

'I'm sorry,' Bob repeated. 'Is there some way the school can help?'

'We're managing,' Pip assured him. 'At least, I thought we were. I guess I haven't been taking as much notice of Alice as I should have been in regard to homework and so on.'

'Let's see how things go now that you're aware of the situation,' Bob suggested. 'And, please, keep in touch and let us know if you need any support.' He opened a drawer in his desk and extracted a pink mobile phone. 'I'll give this to you,' he said to Pip. 'It might be a good idea if Alice restricts its use to out-of-school hours.'

'Can I have my phone back?'

'Not right now. I want to talk to you.'

'It's *my* phone!'

'Alice.' Pip's tone was a warning. She had no intention of being deflected from having a proper discussion with Alice on the drive home. 'This isn't like you. What *is* your problem?'

'School sucks,' Alice declared. 'Nona's sick and you've got a boyfriend. It's *boring*.'

The confrontational tone angered Pip, which made it easy to override the warning bell that suggested she should investigate any effect her relationship with Toni might be having.

'So you thought you'd make life more interesting by getting into trouble at school?'

'It's not as though I've been suspended or anything. It's no big deal.'

'It felt like a big deal to me.'

'Dayna's mother gets called into school all the time. For nothing!'

Bob Henley was hardly likely to waste his time like that. Pip listened to that warning bell this time. She had ignored it when Toni had jokingly suggested that Alice's new friend might be 'cool' in the way Catherine had been 'cool'. Trouble.

'I've never met Dayna, have I?'

'Why should you?'

'You get to meet *my* friends.'

'You mean Toni? Like he'd be hard to miss! He practically lives at our house.'

Pip bit back a defensive comment about how much help Toni had been in the last few weeks. Making him seem more important to her than Alice at the moment wasn't going to help.

'Why don't you ask Dayna round one day? For dinner, perhaps. You could both get some homework done and make your teachers a lot happier.'

Alice snorted. 'Yeah…like *that* would be fun.'

Pip had had enough. 'None of us are having much "fun" at the moment, Alice. Especially Nona. You might like to start thinking about someone other than yourself for a change.'

'Are you saying I'm selfish?'

'I'm saying that it would be nice if you tried helping, instead of trying to make things harder. I'm trying to do everything right now, Alice. My job, the housework, looking after Nona, looking after *you*, and you're not exactly helping. It's hard enough, OK? *Too* hard, even.'

'It's not *my* fault Nona's sick.'

'I'm not saying it is.'

'And it's not as if she's going to *die* or anything.'

Pip steered the car to the side of the road and pulled to a halt. She sat there, aware of Alice's surprised silence, her hands gripping the top of the steering-wheel.

'Actually,' she said, very quietly, turning her head to make eye contact with her daughter, 'she *is*.'

The look in Alice's eyes was awful. Shock.

Mistrust. The silence ticked on and on and then Alice gave a strange sort of hiccup.

'But...but she's just had an operation. Like last time.'

'Not like last time.' Pip steeled herself to maintain the eye contact. 'That's what Nona wanted you to think but she's a lot sicker this time. She's got cancer, Alice. Of her pancreas.'

'Her pancreas!' Pip could see the pupils in Alice's eyes dilating. 'But *I* might have to have an operation, too. Is that what *I've* really got? *Cancer?*'

'No.' She couldn't blame Alice for instantly relating this news to herself. Or for being so afraid. Shona had been right in thinking she would. Had Toni been wrong in advising that she needed to hear the truth? 'You definitely don't have cancer, Alice,' Pip said firmly. 'That's one of the first things they looked for in all those tests you had.'

Alice's eyes were swimming with tears. 'Is Nona really going to die?'

The tears were contagious. 'I'm afraid so, hon.'

'When?'

'We don't know. I hope she'll still be here when you start high school next year, but there are no guarantees. It'll depend on how well the treatment she's getting at the moment works.'

Pip undid her safety belt so she could lean over and hug Alice. 'We need to be as brave as we can,' she said brokenly, 'for Nona's sake. She doesn't want us to be sad. She's wants us all to make the most of whatever time we've got left together. And I...I need your help, hon.'

Would appealing to Alice in a more mature way make any difference?

'Can you do that? Try and help?'

Alice was sobbing now, her face buried against Pip's shoulder.

'I'll...try...'

'Good girl.' Pip kissed the top of her head. 'Love you.'

'You did the right thing.'

'I'm not so sure. She's been so quiet for the last couple of days and she's avoiding spending much time with Mum.'

'Has she been in any more trouble at school?'

'Not that I'm aware of.'

'And she's doing her homework?' Toni could see that some of the tension was leaving Pip's body. She took another sip of her wine and nodded.

'Seems to be.'

'And helping?'

'She did the dishes last night without even being asked.'

'That's better.' Toni traced the outline of Pip's cheek with the back of his index finger. 'You almost smiled then, *bella.*'

'Oh-h.'

Toni loved the way that line of consternation appeared between Pip's eyes. A line he could almost always smooth away.

'Do I seem that miserable?' Pip asked anxiously. 'I'm not, really. Mum's feeling so much better at the moment.'

'That's good.' And it was, but Toni hadn't seen Pip for three days and he had some other things on his mind. Like getting her to relax. Taking her to his bed, finding that magic place where they were so close—body and soul—that he couldn't imagine ever wanting to be anywhere else.

'She's wondering why Alice is so quiet, though.'

'Shona doesn't know that Alice knows the truth?'

'No. I've been scared to tell her. I didn't exactly promise not to but I think Mum assumes I did.'

'You still did the right thing.' Toni picked up Pip's hand and pressed his lips to her palm. 'The only thing you could do as a responsible parent.'

'I wish I felt more like a parent. Like I *knew* that I was doing the right thing.'

'No parent knows that for sure. You just have to do the best you can. What feels right.'

As he would. How many times in the years to come would he sit with Pip like this and reassure her that she had done the right thing? That *they* were doing their best as parents? It would depend entirely on how many children they had, of course.

Toni wanted a lot. At least four. Even six. A happy, noisy tribe of youngsters like some of his schoolmates had had. Theirs would be lucky enough to have a much older and probably adored sister in Alice. Increasingly, Toni had felt the empty space around him in his house and garden. He had imagined it filled with the sound of children's voices and laughter. Had imagined coming home each night knowing that Pip would be there.

Waiting for him.

Loving him.

Not that he was about to rush into proposing marriage or anything. It was enough, for now, to know his trust in Pip had not been misplaced. That the recent weeks, while hardly romantic in the way he would like them to have been, had cemented the depth of how he felt about this woman.

How much he loved her.

It wasn't the right time to talk about their own future. To make plans for a wedding or their own *bambinos*. Not while Pip had to deal with such a crisis in her life. Toni knew he had no right to feel impatient or to put any pressure on Pip, but he couldn't prevent the smile that crept onto his face or resist the need to hold eye contact with the woman he loved and communicate the deep emotion warming his heart.

Pip smiled back. 'You look happy, anyway. Did you have a good day?'

'No, it was terrible! Far too busy. A case of meningitis, two cases of gastroenteritis, one of whom was severely dehydrated. And a little girl with periorbital cellulitis who couldn't even open her eyes, poor thing, so everything was even more terrifying.'

'*Staphylococcus aureus* infection?'

'Yes. And I got called in because my registrar couldn't get near her to get an IV line in. The mother was just as distressed as the child by then.'

'I'm sure you sorted it out.' The way Pip was looking at him made Toni feel on top of the world. Capable of achieving anything and being damn proud of it.

'We gave her some sedation,' he admitted.

Pip's smile broadened. 'Who—the child or the mother?'

'Are you suggesting I need to sedate the relatives in order to treat my patients?' It was so good to see Pip smiling properly. To make her happy. Maybe she was finally in a mental space where he could ease her away from her family responsibilities, at least temporarily.

'I'm sure it would make life a lot easier.'

'My life is exactly the way I want it.' The moment Toni had been waiting for ever since Pip had arrived at his house that evening was finally here. He could lean close enough to kiss her still smiling lips. And he did. Slowly. Tenderly.

The need to say something else was an unwanted distraction so he barely pulled back. He could still feel the softness of Pip's mouth beneath his as he spoke.

'*Exactly* the way I want it,' he whispered.

With a sigh of pure contentment Toni focused completely on making love to the first woman who had ever captured his soul as well as his mind and body. Minutes later, with no protest from Pip, he scooped her into his arms and carried her away to his bedroom.

'Are you seeing Toni again tonight?'

'He's coming round soon. He said something about a challenge you'd issued regarding Scrabble?' Pip eyed her mother suspiciously. 'Since when did you become a Scrabble fanatic?'

'Since I found what a good distraction it is,' Shona responded. She grinned. 'I'm such a good speller. I can cane everybody.'

'Hmm. Do you need another cushion?'

'No.' Shona was stretched out on the couch in the living room. 'This is perfect.'

'Are you warm enough?'

'I'm fine. Stop fussing, love.'

'Have you taken all your pills?'

'It's a wonder I had room for any dinner after that lot.'

'You didn't have room for much.' Pip glanced at her watch. It was only 6.30 p.m. They had eaten earlier than usual because Alice had been hungry. 'It's about time for your insulin.'

'Bring me the box. I'd like to do it for myself tonight.'

'You'll need to test your blood-glucose level first so we can check the dose.'

'I can do that.' Shona sounded irritated now. 'I'm not stupid, Philippa.'

'I know that.' Pip backed off. 'You wouldn't cane everybody at Scrabble if that were the case.' She went to the kitchen, returning with the container of drugs, syringes and the testing kit. 'You might even beat Toni later.'

'As long as he doesn't claim international privilege and throw in Italian words, like he did last time.' Shona took the container. 'Where's Alice?' She didn't like her granddaughter having to see her have injections.

'She's in her room, doing her homework.'

'She seems to be working very hard lately. She didn't even argue much when you said she couldn't go to the mall with Dayna.'

'There's no way I'd let her wander around the mall for no reason on a school night. It's just asking for trouble.'

'I agree, but it does seem to be what most teenagers want to do these days. Especially on late-shopping nights. And Alice has seemed very keen to spend as much time as possible with her friends lately.'

'Maybe getting into trouble at school was just what she needed to pull her socks up.'

'Hmm.' Shona wasn't convinced. 'So why am I getting the impression it's a good excuse to avoid *me*?'

'I don't know.'

'Yes, you do.'

The tone was one well remembered from childhood and with a small, defeated sigh Pip lowered herself to sit on the arm of the couch. 'I had to tell her the truth, Mum. I'm sorry. Things were just getting out of hand.'

Shona was silent for a long moment. 'I suppose she had to know,' she said eventually.

'Yes. Toni thought it was the right thing to do.'

'A shame it had to be this soon, though. When I'm starting to feel a bit better. Like I might even win this battle for a while, anyway.'

'I know. But she asked, kind of, and I couldn't lie.'

'No.' Shona leaned back on her cushions, her eyes closed. 'I'll talk to her so it's all out in the open. I knew there something going on that I didn't know about.'

'I should have told you. I'm not dealing with any this particularly well, am I?'

'You're doing just fine. None of it is easy—for any of us. We'll get used to it.'

'I'm not so sure about that. About managing

this parenting bit by myself. I just don't feel, you know, maternal enough, I guess.'

Shona smiled. 'It takes practice.'

'I'm not sure I can do any of it without you to back me up,' Pip said sadly. 'I was a complete failure as a parent right from the start with Alice, wasn't I?'

'You were sixteen,' Shona said, as though that explained everything.

But it didn't. Plenty of sixteen-year-olds had babies and felt the kind of instant bond you were supposed to feel with your baby, didn't they? They wouldn't have been so relieved that someone more maternal was there to fill the breach and gradually take full responsibility.

'It'll be different next time,' Shona said. 'You'll see.'

'No, I won't,' Pip said fervently. 'There's not going to be a "next time".' Even now, the terror of those long, pain-filled hours of labour was a memory clear enough to make the hairs on the back of Pip's neck prickle. And that had only been the start. The feeling of inadequacy—of failing to be a good parent—had been unpleasant and ongoing. It seemed to be surfacing with a new regularity all over again now—like during that interview with Alice's headmaster.

'Doesn't Toni want children?'

'He's never mentioned it.'

'He seems very happy to include Alice in your relationship.'

'Yes. He's great with children, which is partly why he's such a brilliant paediatrician. Plus, he's Italian. They all seem to adore kids and realise how important families are.' Pip felt a familiar wave of gratitude. How many women in her position would be lucky enough to find a lover who would take on board an older child and a sick mother they weren't related to?

'So don't you think he's going to want a family of his own?'

'Maybe not. He didn't have a very happy childhood himself. That can be enough to stop people wanting to have their own children.'

'And it can make others want to undo the damage by making sure it doesn't happen to the next generation.' Shona was watching Pip now, her expression anxious. 'You're still so young, darling. You could easily have more children.'

'But I don't want to.'

And she didn't want to talk about it any more. It wasn't just the thought of being expected to have more children that was disturbing, it was that the thought hadn't occurred to her prior to this. Maybe it was an issue she should have discussed with Toni right at the start of their relationship. But then, how could she have known how intense things were going to get? On her part, at any rate. She still didn't know how Toni really felt. Whether he was considering a real commitment to a future together. This wasn't the time to be thinking about it, anyway. She had far too much else going on in her life.

'Sometimes you have to be prepared to compromise if you want a relationship to work,' Shona said.

'Hmm.' The sound was noncommittal but it wasn't an area that was up for negotiation as far as Pip was concerned. She wasn't about to prove herself a failure all over again. It was time to change the subject. 'Are you sure you don't want some help with that insulin?'

'I'm sure.' But Shona wasn't about to let Pip close the subject quite yet. 'Talk to him about it, won't you, Pip?'

'Of course I will. Sometime. It's early days, Mum.'

'Not for me,' Shona said quietly. She summoned a smile for her daughter. 'Don't take this the wrong way, love. It's just that I'd like to think I'm going to be around long enough to help plan a wedding rather than a funeral.'

Why couldn't life be simple?

The information contained in the article Pip was reading in an emergency medicine journal on the management of secondary deterioration in level of consciousness wasn't really sinking in.

She had declined another game of Scrabble, having been soundly beaten by both Toni and Shona, who were happily engaged in another epic battle. The Scrabble board sat on a small table beside the couch and Toni's long frame was lounging on the floor on its other side. Pip could see he had way too many vowels on his letter rack but he seemed undaunted.

'Axe,' he said aloud. 'Ten points.'

How homely was this? All it needed to complete the picture of happy domesticity would be to have Alice doing her homework on the dining table in the corner of the room, instead of being shut away in her bedroom at the other end of the house.

Inclusion couldn't be forced, though, and the niggling worry that Alice resented Toni's inclusion in her mother's life was just one of the underlying tensions that made the happy picture only superficial.

Pip tried to return her attention to the article. Constant reassessment of level of consciousness was mandatory, she read, as changes in the Glasgow coma score were more important than any static assessment. Faced with deterioration, the first objective was to confirm oxygenation and ventilatory adequacy. Then to ensure adequate volume status and haemoglobin. And to check BGL.

The mention of a blood-sugar level was enough to make Pip glance towards the couch again.

'Extra,' Shona was pronouncing with satisfaction. 'I used your "x", Toni, only I got it on a triple word.'

'Very good,' Toni said with a feigned level of grudging admiration. 'What's the score?'

'Twenty-two.'

'Really? It should be more than that.' He leaned over the board. 'It's more like thirty-six!'

It was so good to see her mother looking this happy. The tension of worrying about her condition and managing all the hurdles they were bound to face in the coming months was the biggest reason that life was nowhere near simple. It occurred to Pip that Shona might be looking this happy right now because she was with someone who wasn't as emotionally involved as she was herself. Someone who could operate better in that superficial picture and treat Shona as though she was going to be around to play Scrabble for many years.

Was it a reprieve for her mother—in the way that it was for Pip when *she* spent special time with Toni?

Like last night had been.

Impossible to concentrate on information about criteria for consulting a neurosurgical team and ordering urgent cerebral scanning for someone whose level of consciousness was dropping. Pip's head was firmly where her body had been last night. Being loved so thoroughly—so *amazingly*—by Toni Costa.

Thanks to that earlier conversation with Shona, however, a new tension had been added to the complexity of Pip's life. Was her mother's notion, that Toni would definitely want his own children something she should add to her list of worries? Or could it be shelved, in the same way as that niggle about Alice resenting her attachment to someone new?

If it wasn't broken, don't try and fix it, she told herself.

Things were fragile enough without searching for cracks, weren't they?

Maybe managing life was the same as being a parent. You dealt with things when you had to. You did what felt right and you did the best you could. Addressing issues that weren't an obvious problem and could be potentially destructive certainly didn't feel like the right thing to do.

Pip discarded her journal. 'Anybody feel like a hot drink? Tea or coffee?'

'Please.' Toni had his gaze on the board. '"Predom" is not a word,' he said to Shona. 'Sorry.'

'It is, too.'

Pip laughed. 'Of course it isn't. Do you want the dictionary, Mum?'

'Don't need it. I can spell.'

'Do you want a cup of tea?'

'Yes. Go away.'

'I'll come and help you.' Toni pushed himself up off the floor. 'You can have another go while I'm gone, if you like, Shona.'

'Don't need it.'

'Is she serious?' Toni asked when they had reached the privacy of the kitchen. 'I'm right, aren't I? Or is "predom" some English word I haven't learned yet?'

'It's not a word,' Pip assured him. 'Mum's just getting stroppy. She's probably tired.' She filled the electric kettle and switched it on.

'Are you tired, *cara*?'

'Not really.'

'Good. Come here, then.'

Pip was only too willing to go into his open arms. To raise her face for one of the kisses she was coming to know so well. Kisses that she couldn't imagine not receiving on a very regular basis.

It took some time for them to complete the task of setting a tray for supper, but Pip felt happier than she had all day by the time they returned to the living room.

'Here's your tea, Mum. Do you feel like a biscuit?' Pip peered at her mother before turning to Toni. 'I think you tired her out. She's too sleepy for a hot drink.'

'Hmm.' Toni came closer. 'Shona?'

'Don't wake her,' Pip advised. 'She needs a rest.'

'Hmm,' Toni said again. He laid his hand on Shona's forehead. 'She's very clammy,' he said. This time Pip said nothing as he shook Shona's shoulder. 'Shona? Wake up!'

'I'll get her blood-glucose monitor,' Pip said. 'Maybe she wasn't just being stroppy with that strange word.'

'She certainly looks like she could be hypoglycaemic,' Toni agreed. 'She's diaphoretic and tachycardic and she's quite deeply unconscious. I'm going to call an ambulance.'

Pip was back with the kit rapidly. 'She insisted on doing her insulin herself tonight.'

'What was her BGL reading?'

'It says 8.4 on this but that's what it was this morning. It's been so unstable lately I'd be very surprised if it had been the same this evening. Maybe she forgot to take it.' Pip had inserted the test strip. She used a lancet to prick the end of her mother's finger and then collected a drop of blood on the end of the strip.

The wail of an ambulance siren could be heard in the distance by the time they got proof that Shona's blood-sugar level was dangerously low.

While the paramedics established IV access and started a glucose infusion running, Pip sped down the hall and knocked on Alice's door.

'Alice?'

She opened the door to find Alice lying on her bed with headphones on. Compact discs were scattered all around her and even from where she stood, Pip could hear the music. Alice jumped at the intrusion and peeled the head-phones off.

'What?' she demanded. 'I've finished my homework.'

'Nona's sick,' Pip said tersely. 'We're going to take her into the hospital by ambulance. Do you want to come with us?'

Alice went very pale. 'Is she…?'

'No, hon, it's OK.' Pip's heart squeezed pain-fully as she saw the level of distress in Alice's face. 'It looks like she might have had too much insulin tonight but it should be easy enough to fix. We just need to have her in hospital to make sure we get it right and an ambulance is the most comfortable way for her to travel.'

'Will you be gone all night?'

'No. I'll come home as soon as things are stable.'

'Then can I stay here? I don't like hospitals and I want to watch TV later.'

'Would you be all right by yourself? I could ask Mary to come over.'

'I'll be fine.' Alice sat up on the edge of her bed. 'I'm not a kid any more, Pip. I don't need a babysitter.'

'OK.' It was much easier to relate to Alice when she wanted to be treated more as an adult than a child. 'I'll call you soon, then.'

The phone call went unanswered an hour later when Pip was finally happy to leave her mother's bedside.

'I'm perfectly all right,' Shona was insisting. 'But I'm not hungry. I really don't want that sandwich.'

'You need to try and eat it, Mum. It's part of the management for an insulin overdose.'

'It wasn't an overdose. I just had a bit of trouble with the monitor. I couldn't get it to beep when I put the test strip in.'

'It was probably the wrong way round.'

'I'll get it right next time.'

Pip thought that her phone call home would be answered the next time she tried, but it wasn't. She tried Alice's mobile phone but it went straight to voicemail.

'She's probably got her headphones on again,' Toni said. 'With the music loud enough to deafen her.'

'I'm still worried. I think I'll call a taxi and head home. They're going to keep Mum in overnight to monitor her blood-glucose levels.'

'I'll come with you.'

It wasn't late when they arrived back at the Murdochs' house—a little after 9 p.m. and Pip fully expected to find Alice curled up in her bed watching television.

She could hear the telephone ringing as she unlocked the front door, but it stopped as soon as she stepped into the hallway.

'I wonder who that was at this time of night?'

Toni was close behind her. 'If it was important, they'll ring again.'

'I hope it wasn't the hospital.'

'They'll have your mobile number.'

'Yes.' Pip stopped talking, aware of how quiet the house was. She couldn't hear the sound of a television. She couldn't hear anything.

'Alice?' she called. 'We're home.'

The silence was more than just a quiet house. It felt…empty.

The living room was empty, the Scrabble

board with its unfinished game a reminder of how much the evening's peace had been disrupted. Pip kept moving. The bathroom light was on but the small space was deserted. An open mascara wand lay beside the basin. Pip's bedroom was in darkness, the screen of the portable television blank, but there was a light showing under Alice's door.

Pip knocked once and opened the door. 'Alice?'

Seconds later, she entered the kitchen where Toni was busy making coffee.

'Toni?'

He turned swiftly. 'What's up, *cara*?'

'Alice isn't here.'

'She must be,'

Pip shook her head in bewilderment. 'I've checked everywhere. She's not here.'

'Where could she have gone?'

'I don't know.' A dreadful sensation was gripping Pip. She shouldn't have left Alice at home alone. She was really only a child still. What kind of parent would do something like that?

Pip had no idea at all of where Alice might be or who she might be with. She had failed—yet again—to do the right thing as a parent, and this time she might have put her daughter into real danger.

'Oh, my God, Toni,' Pip breathed. 'What am I going to do?'

Toni's touch was reassuring. At least she wasn't going to be alone in tackling whatever new crisis was about to present itself in her life. He opened his mouth to say something but, at exactly the same moment, the telephone began to ring again.

Pip froze. This was going to be bad news, she just knew it.

Toni looked at her face. 'I'll answer that,' he said. He touched her cheek. 'I'll be right back.'

CHAPTER SEVEN

'WE'LL be right there.' Toni put the phone down and turned to Pip. 'She's safe.'

'But where *is* she?'

'With the police.'

'What?' Horrific images of abduction and potential violence crowded the back of Pip's mind.

'She's safe,' Toni repeated. 'She's at the mall.'

'I don't understand.'

'She and her friend—Daisy, is it?'

'Dayna?'

'Yes. They were caught shoplifting.'

'Oh, no!' Pip groaned. 'How *could* they?'

'They're too young to be arrested but apparently the mall's policy is to involve the police. They want you to go and collect Alice.'

Pip nodded tersely. She scooped up her car

keys from the bowl on the end of the kitchen bench. ' I'll go straight away.'

'I'm coming with you.'

'You don't have to do that, Toni.' Pip's half-smile was rueful. 'As if you haven't had enough of my family's dramas for one evening.'

'I'm not going to let you cope with this by yourself, Pippa.' Toni patted the pocket of his jacket and Pip heard the rattle of keys. 'I'll drive.'

The strength that Toni's company imparted was dented as soon as they entered the mall management's offices.

'What's *he* doing here?' Alice demanded.

'Who is he?' The girl sitting beside Alice had bleached, blonde hair, too much make-up and a top that exposed several inches of midriff and a large jewel in a belly-button piercing.

'My mother's boyfriend.'

'Oh-h. So that's the Italian stallion.'

The derogatory tone and the innuendo was too much for Pip. So was the sullen expression on the girl's face. At least Alice had the sense to look frightened beneath a thin layer of defiance, faced as she was with the presence of a bored-looking security guard, an angry mall management representative and two police officers.

Pip would have expected her to be looking relieved with the arrival of someone prepared to defend her, but Alice didn't look any more pleased to see her mother than Toni.

'You're Alice Murdoch's mother?' The police-woman looked surprised.

'Yes.' Pip was in no mood to provide an explanation for looking too young for the part.

'She's been spotted in the mall on several occasions, so we're told—with Dayna here. The security guard followed up his suspicions tonight and kept a close eye on the pair of them.'

The nod from the burly security guard was satisfied.

'These items were found in Dayna's bag as they were trying to leave the mall at closing time.'

Several items of clothing were lying on the office desk, the labels advertising their newness.

Toni raised his eyebrows. 'So Alice hasn't actually stolen anything?'

'She was aware of what was going on. A willing accomplice.'

Alice wasn't meeting Pip's gaze so she turned to the policewoman. 'What's going to happen to her?'

'At this stage, probably nothing more than a warning, but we wanted you to be aware of what your daughter's involved in, Mrs Murdoch. It's not the first time we've had trouble with her friend, Dayna, and we intend to deal with her a lot more severely. If you don't want future involvement with the police and Social Services, I suggest you take your daughter home and have a very serious discussion with her.'

'Oh, I will,' Pip said heavily. 'Don't worry.'

Extra stress like this was the last thing they needed at this time. The thought of having to explain all this to Shona was horrible. Why was Alice choosing now to make trouble? To emphasise *her* failure to meet the demands of taking over as a full-time parent? Pip felt as though she was under siege.

'How long has this sort of thing been going on?' she snapped as they marched Alice towards the car a short time later.

Alice shrugged.

'Those CDs and videos and everything that Dayna's been lending you lately—are they all stolen property?'

Another shrug was infuriating.

'Do you *want* to get into real trouble?' Pip's voice rose. 'End up in juvenile court and get suspended from school?'

Alice's silence continued as they climbed into the car. It was Toni who broke it as he started the engine. 'I think the problem might be one of association rather than intent,' he said mildly.

Pip was hoping that was true. She could deal with that. 'You're not to have anything more to do with Dayna,' she informed Alice crisply. 'She's bad news.'

'She's my *friend*.'

'What kind of friend sets out to get you into big trouble?'

'Why should you care?'

'Because I'm your *mother*, that's why!'

'No, you're not.'

Shocked by the vehement tone, Pip turned to look at Alice. The intermittent light from streetlamps couldn't conceal a very adult anger on the young girl's face.

'You've never been my mother,' Alice continued bitterly. 'Not really. You never wanted me. You couldn't even look after me by yourself. Nona had to do it.'

Pip could sense the glance she was getting from Toni without meeting it. He was as shocked as she was. He might want to help but there was nothing he could do or say. This was between Pip and Alice and it was private. He was probably embarrassed to be a witness. Pip was certainly embarrassed. Mortified, even. She'd always felt a failure as a parent but she'd never expected such blatant confirmation of her inadequacy to come from her child.

The despair in Alice's voice filled the car. 'Now Nona's going to die and she's the only person who ever cared about me.'

'That's *not* true, Alice.' The despair her daughter was feeling was an abyss that Pip had no idea how to reach across. The distance felt impossible. 'I love you. I've *always* loved you.'

'You gave me to Nona. You went back to

school and then you went away to university. For years and years and *years.*'

What could she say to that? It was true. They had discussed moving so that they could live in a city that boasted a medical school, but it would have meant all the upheaval of selling and buying a new house in a far more expensive area, and finances had been tight enough as it was. Alice would have been taken away from the play centre she'd loved. From the GP who had cared for her since birth. Shona would have lost her own friends, who'd provided a network of support. And they'd decided against it because Alice had been so happy.

Pip had been so sure that she had been the only one to suffer because of the prolonged absences.

'I missed you,' she told Alice. The words sounded totally pathetic. 'I always told you how much I missed you.'

'Ha!' The sound was derisive. 'It's not as if anything changed even when you came back. You're always working now. You still don't want me. I'm just in the way.'

'That's *not* true!'

'You've got Toni,' Alice said accusingly. 'You'll get married now and have babies that you *do* want. You'll forget all about me.'

'*No!*' Pip put all the conviction she could into the word. She had to ignore the sharp intake of breath from Toni. This wasn't the time to try and explain she was denying a lack of interest in Alice rather than the prospect of marriage or babies with Toni. 'That's not going to happen, Alice.'

'And I'll have no one.' Alice either hadn't heard or didn't believe her.

The car had stopped. They were home. And it had never felt less like home.

Toni switched off the engine and spoke for the first time since they'd left the mall car park. 'You're not going to lose your mother, Alice. She loves you. I know you're going through a tough time at the moment and I understand how you feel. I—'

'Shut *up!*' Alice shouted. 'You don't know anything. This is *your* fault, anyway.'

'Alice!' Pip couldn't help the remonstrative exclamation but, it was lost in Alice's continued shouting.

'We were fine before you came along. Now Nona's going to die and Mummy doesn't have time for me any more and…and I *hate* you.'

Pip tried again. 'Alice, you can't say that.'

'I can, too.' Alice was fumbling with the door catch. 'It's true. And I hate you, too. Go away. Go and live with Toni and have babies and see if I care.'

'I'm not going to do that, Alice.'

'I don't *care*!' Alice flung the door open and jumped out. She was crying now but still managed to shout between the racking sobs. 'Have *lots* of babies. Sing them all the special ottipuss song. I. Don't. *Care*!'

Stunned, Pip got out of the car. Alice had left the front door wide open and she heard her daughter's bedroom door slamming as she entered the house.

'Let her go,' Toni advised quietly. 'She's not going to hear anything you want to say to her until she's had time to calm down a little.'

He was probably right but it went against every instinct Pip had. She needed to hold her child. To rock her. To reassure her that she was deeply loved. And wanted. And she *would* do that—just as soon as Alice would let her close enough.

Until then it seemed to be Pip's turn to be held and comforted but, for the first time, it didn't feel right to be in Toni's arms. There was something a little stiff and awkward about the embrace— almost as if they were strangers. His body felt tense. Clearly, he was upset as well. When Pip went to pull away, Toni released her instantly. So fast, in fact, that Pip had to wonder if he'd let go even before she'd started to move.

Was he upset at simply being involved in this horrible conflict between her and Alice? More than that? Oh…yes. Pip remembered that shocked sound from him when he'd taken more than she intended from her words of reassurance to Alice. But he couldn't really expect her to want to think about or discuss the future right now, would he? Whether it was possible she would ever want another child when this had to be the time she'd felt more of a failure as a parent than ever before?

'I had *no* idea,' she said slowly, closing the front door behind them, 'that Alice felt anything like that.'

'I do understand where she's coming from, even if Alice doesn't believe me,' Toni said soberly. 'I've always hated my own mother for not wanting me.'

'But I *did* want Alice.' To have Toni taking Alice's side was almost as shocking as her daughter's attack had been. She turned swiftly to face him. 'I know I needed a lot of help looking after her, but I was only sixteen, for God's sake! And it wasn't my idea to go back to school and then to go to university. I got talked into it and there didn't seem to be a good enough reason not to go. Alice was too young to understand the difference between the people who loved her and looked after her. She was *happy*.'

'She's not very happy at the moment.'

Rubbing that in was cruel. And unnecessary. Pip could suddenly understand Alice shouting at Toni. She barely stopped herself doing the same. The bubble of responsibility she felt for upsetting Toni evaporated. So did any intention of trying to discuss this from his perspective. Of telling him she hadn't meant to deny the chance of a future together. She couldn't think of anyone but Alice right now.

'Of course she's not happy,' she said with tight control. 'Her grandmother's dying. She's trying to find a way of dealing with that and it's too much for her. She's sad and angry and looking for someone to blame. *Me.*'

Pip's control slipped and she buried her face in her hands. 'I shouldn't have told her the truth. Not yet. Mum was right—she's got too many things changing all at once.'

Alice wasn't the only one with too many things changing all at once.

Toni stood there in the hallway near the front door, wanting to take Pip in his arms to try and reassure her, but what if she just pulled away like she had only moments ago?

It was hard not to feel rejected with that vehement declaration of Alice's still ringing in his ears.

She hated him.

And a phrase Pip had uttered was vying for equal prominence.

'That's not going to happen,' she'd said.

What wasn't going to happen? At the time Toni

had dismissed the shock of her words and assumed Pip was reassuring Alice that her daughter was still going to be important in her life, no matter what. A part of her new family if she did marry Toni and they had their own children.

But right now, as Toni stood with his arms by his sides, miserably checking the impulse to hold Pip—in the wake of her pulling away from his comfort—that first meaning that had occurred to him seemed far more likely to be the correct one..

What wasn't going to happen was a future with him.

Was it possible he had made a terrible mistake?

That he'd given away so much of his heart to Pip that it could never be whole again if she wasn't in his life and that she didn't feel the same way about him? And never would?

The seconds ticked past. Awkward seconds. Pip had taken her hands from her face and had been staring in the direction Alice had taken down the hallway towards the bedrooms. When she looked up at Toni, her expression was desolate.

'She blames me for everything. I've messed things up completely, haven't I?'

'No.' Toni's smile was wry. 'It's all *my* fault, remember? Alice hates me.'

'She hates me, too.'

For bringing Toni into her life on top of everything else Alice perceived that Pip had done wrong as a parent.

A flash of something akin to amusement showed in Pip's eyes. They were both hated, which could actually deepen the bond between them. Except that Pip couldn't afford to let that happen, could she? Not if she didn't see a future together. Not if she wanted to repair the damage in her relationship with her daughter.

'No.' Toni spoke more seriously this time. 'It's me that Alice is really resenting. She needs you and she sees me as competition. Me being here is making things harder…for you all.'

Would Pip try and reassure him in some way? Perhaps even give them the chance to discuss that damning denial of the future he'd been dreaming of with the sound of small feet and happy laughter filling his house?

He wanted to touch her. To remind her how much he loved her, but that would be begging for reassurance, wouldn't it? For the sake of his pride as much as not wanting to force the issue, Toni had to make himself wait for Pip's response.

A response that was slow in coming.

Too slow.

She certainly wasn't inclined to grasp the opportunity to silence that negative little voice in his head that was replaying things said under duress. He was upset as well and Pip's silence stirred the unpleasant emotion enough to make him go a step further.

'Maybe you need some time as a family. The way you used to be. Without me.'

Pip was staring at him but he couldn't read her expression. Couldn't find the reassurance that his offer might not be welcome. And it hurt.

She must know that he was doing more than offering her some space. That he was really asking if she wanted him as part of her life.

If she wanted *him*.

Pip opened her mouth to speak but then had to close it again. What could she say? She had feared this moment would come. That her baggage would become too much of a burden and that Toni would want to distance himself.

This was the perfect opportunity, wasn't it? Alice had made it very clear that she resented Toni and his relationship with her mother. He would have to be very determined that he wanted a future with her to weather a storm like this.

If she told him what she wanted to say—that she couldn't imagine being able to cope without the kind of strength he gave her—would it come across as being needy and scare him even further away?

Or, worse, would it open the can of worms regarding how he saw their future if he did stay to help her through yet another family crisis? If he told her that having his own family was paramount, it would add a new pressure. An additional facet to the emotional forces laying siege to her life. Pip couldn't handle that.

Not tonight.

And maybe Toni was offering this space because that was what he wanted himself. An escape. And why wouldn't he? Pip could see this from his point of view so easily. His own mother had failed him miserably. He was currently in a ringside seat to observe Pip's failure with her own daughter. Would he wish that on any children of his own? Not likely.

But could Pip summon the dignity to let him have that escape if that was what he was really asking for? Could she do it in a civilised fashion even?

'I do need to talk to Alice,' she said finally. 'To try and make her understand.'

'Of course. I'll go home.'

'I'll see you tomorrow?' Pip couldn't help sounding hopeful. 'At work?'

'Of course.' Toni paused, his fingers gripping the doorhandle. His smile seemed different. Distant. Then he raised an eyebrow. 'What did Alice mean?' he asked, 'by the "special ottipuss" song?'

'I used to sing to her to get her to sleep when she a baby,' Pip responded softly. 'It was a Beatles' song—"The Octopus's Garden". Only she was too little to be able to pronounce it.'

'How old was she?'

'Less than two.' Pip had stopped singing that

song after she'd gone away to medical school. 'I'm amazed she remembers it.'

'Some things are never forgotten, Pippa.'

So true. Like the look Toni was giving her right now. An uncomfortable look as though he was upset because he knew he might be hurting her by walking out like this but couldn't help himself. He needed to escape.

She had to be strong.

She had to think about Alice right now.

Her *daughter*.

Part of herself. A part that was torn and bleeding right now. A part that had nothing to do with Toni, no matter how much she loved him.

Why hadn't she heeded those warnings that Alice resented how quickly and deeply Toni had become part of their lives? No wonder she felt shut out and unable to cope with Shona's illness. How selfish had Pip been, letting her relationship become so important?

As selfish as she'd been pursuing the career she'd dreamed of and letting her mother shoulder ninety per cent of the upbringing of her young child?

No wonder Alice had felt the need to attack her.

For being an inadequate mother.

For appearing to abandon Alice for the second time in her short life. For choosing an education and now for choosing a lover—at the worst possible time—when Alice needed her more than she ever had.

It felt wrong to Pip to be standing here like this, debating whether there was anything else she could say to Toni that would make him—and herself—feel better. She had almost made a joke of Alice hating them both equally—as though they were both her real parents. She should be trying to get through to Alice even if there was no hope of succeeding just yet. Otherwise, Alice could accuse her of not caring enough to even try.

Something else was hurting, too, quite apart from the thought that Toni was pulling away from their relationship. His query about that long discarded song had evoked a powerful memory. Another one of those things that could never be forgotten.

The memory of holding a tiny, warm, sweet-smelling body. The tickle of soft red-gold curls as Pip bent into the cot to kiss her daughter goodnight.

The feeling of the bond that had always been there but had been buried under layers of unwelcome feelings. Of being inadequate. Too young. Too alone. Too uneducated.

None of those excuses held water any more.

Except maybe being alone because Toni was leaving now with no more than a nod of parting.

The click of the front door closing behind him had a finality that completed the downward slide of an evening from hell. One that seemed to have been scripted purely for the purpose of breaking Pip's heart.

CHAPTER EIGHT

THE children's ward had never looked so festive.

The paediatrician heading for the treatment room had never felt so bleak.

'Dr Costa! Look at *me*!'

A tiny child was propelling a custom-built wheelchair at speed along the central corridor of the paediatric ward and came to a halt, barely missing Toni's toes.

The small boy was wearing a Superman costume. The mask was far too big, covering most of his face, but the misshapen body in the chair would have been instantly recognisable in any case.

Toni sounded as puzzled as possible, however. 'Goodness me, who can this be?'

'It's *me*!' The mask was dragged upwards. 'Nathan. See?'

'So it is! I'd never have guessed.'

Nathan beamed at him. He knew perfectly well that his doctor was being less than honest but it was the correct response. The familiar broad grin of this long-term patient was welcome. Nathan had spent far too many of his six years in and out of hospital to deal with the management and complications of his physical abnormalities but he never seemed to resent any of it. His mission in life was clearly to have as much fun as possible and nobody could resist the uplifting effect of his personality.

Even Toni, the way he had been feeling for days now. Ever since Pip had apparently accepted his offer to step out of her life.

'It's Hallowe'en,' Nathan informed Toni. 'And I'm going in the *parade*!'

'So am I.' Eight-year-old Jasmine, sporting a pair of sky-blue fairy wings and wielding a glittery wand in a rather menacing fashion, emerged from the nearby bathroom.

'Cool bananas,' Toni said, still smiling.

This celebration had been planned for weeks. Parents, nurses, physiotherapists, occupational therapists and everybody else concerned with the wellbeing of the children in this ward had been using the calendar date as inspiration to keep their young patients motivated, distracted or just amused. Masks and costumes had been made or hired and all those well enough were going to go on a pre-planned 'trick or treat' parade through carefully primed areas of the hospital such as the geriatric wards, cafeteria, pharmacy, the waiting area of the emergency department and even the chapel.

A baby with a pumpkin hat that took attention away from the dressings covering a recently repaired cleft palate and hare-lip was carried past, and an older girl with a nasal cannula supplying oxygen from a tank she pushed in front of her had the cylinder disguised with a large bunch of straw that had a stick poking up from the centre.

'It's my broom,' she told Toni when he raised his eyebrows.

'You're going as a sweeper, Jodi?'

'No, silly.' Jodi had to catch her breath. The chest infection complicating management of her cystic fibrosis was not yet conquered. 'I'm going to be…a witch. Mum's bringing…my costume.'

Another wheelchair came to clutter the part of the corridor Toni had stopped in and a nurse carrying one of their young arthritic patients, who was looking extra-cute in a tiger suit, shook her head.

'I might have known,' she said. 'If there's a traffic jam of kids anywhere, it'll be Dr Costa in the middle of it.'

Toni eyed her headband that had sparkling red devil's horns attached. 'Very appropriate, Mandy.' He nodded approvingly.

The nurse sniffed. 'I'll find a costume for you, don't worry.'

'That won't be necessary.'

'What? You're not coming on the parade?' Several sets of horrified eyes were glued on Toni.

'Of course I'm coming.' He may not feel anything like as enthusiastic as he managed to sound but the delight displayed by Nathan and his fellow ward members made the effort worthwhile.

'What are you…coming as?' Jodi asked.

'Hmm, let me think.' Toni kept up a thoughtful silence but was uninspired. 'Maybe I could come as…a doctor?' He waggled the end of the stethoscope hanging round his neck but the children all shook their heads sadly.

Mandy giggled. 'You'll have to do better than that.'

Toni was spared any further efforts by another nurse appearing in a nearby doorway.

'We're ready for you, Toni.'

He escaped to the relative security of the treatment room where an anxious mother was waiting, holding a ten-month-old girl.

'You've had this procedure explained to you?' Toni queried.

'Yes. I wish there was a different way to get the urine specimen, though. It seems horrible, having to stick a needle through Emily's stomach.'

'It's a very fine needle,' Toni assured her. 'And a quick procedure. I'll be very gentle.'

'Is it really necessary?'

Toni nodded. 'It's important that we find the source of Emily's infection so we can make sure we've got her on the right antibiotics. This won't take long but she's not going to be happy about us doing it. Would you rather the nurse looked after her and you waited back in Emily's room?'

Relief and worry vied to take over Emily's mother's expression. 'Would that be all right? I'd feel terrible leaving her.'

'If it's going to upset you, then it's probably better for Emily if you're not here. We'll get another nurse to help us and we'll take very good care of her, I promise. You'll be able to give her all the cuddling she needs as soon as it's over.'

The woman burst into tears as she left the room and Toni could sympathise. Most mothers would far rather have a procedure themselves than witness their children suffering. Some, like Emily's mother, found it unbearable, whereas others refused to be parted from their children no matter how dreadful the procedure might be.

The bond between mothers and their children had always fascinated Toni. Perhaps he was more conscious of it than most because the lack of experiencing it personally had always haunted him. He was confident that the awareness had made him a better doctor. He approved of the bond. He went out of his way to support the parents of his small patients.

So he had no right to feel rejected because Pip was putting Alice's needs ahead of his own, had he?

Or to feel resentful of Alice. To feel that she was knowingly depriving him of what he most wanted.

A family.

She wasn't even prepared to acknowledge her mother at the moment. She had no idea how lucky she was to have someone who loved her that much. Someone who was prepared to sacrifice something as important as a relationship with a lover to make things better for her child.

Toni scrubbed his hands at the basin in the treatment room while the nurse jiggled baby Emily, who was grizzling loudly in the wake of her mother's disappearance.

'Could you poke your head out the door, please?' Toni asked. 'See if Mandy or someone is free to help us for a minute. We'll need two people to keep Emily still enough.'

He dried his hands and tried to shake off the downward spiral of his spirits that had begun yet again by thinking about Pip and Alice, but day by day a negative interpretation of their current situation seemed to become more prominent and there didn't seem to be anything he could do about it.

Toni couldn't take the first step, no matter how much he might want to. He couldn't force his way back into Pip's life. What would be the point? She had to *want* him.

If Pip felt anything like the same level of emotion he did, she would find it impossible to exclude him, no matter how powerful the bond with her child was. He could have helped to find another way through this impasse but he hadn't even been given the opportunity. As each day had passed, the feeling of being less than significant in Pip's life had increased.

And something even more negative than the sensation of rejection had blossomed. Betrayal. The kind of betrayal he had sworn never to make himself vulnerable to again. For the first time in his adult life Toni had totally trusted a woman. Had given himself heart and soul. He was missing Pip terribly. A dozen times he had picked up his phone, intending to call or text.

Compelled to jump over that boundary line and find out if she was all right and whether there was any way he could help. Each time, something had stopped him.

And he knew exactly what it was.

The echo of her vehemence in assuring Alice that she had no intention of marrying him or having his babies refused to fade. If anything, it got louder every time it clawed its way back into his head.

'It's not going to happen,' she'd said.

It's *not* going to happen.

Surely Pip would realise the interpretation he could have put on those words? The damage they could have done? Toni was quite prepared to believe the more positive spin of it being a promise to include Alice in their lives, and even the smallest gesture on Pip's part would have been enough to make him feel wanted and repair the damage. Just a phone call. Even a text. Just...contact.

There hadn't been any.

This was the fourth day since Alice had confronted Pip with those awful accusations of being less than a real mother. Shona had been discharged the next day and must be doing well enough for Pip to continue working because he'd seen her car in the car park on more than one occasion. Probably because he'd been looking for it.

Mandy came into the room as Toni snapped on some gloves. 'Thanks, Mandy. We've just got a suprapubic aspiration to do on Emily for a urine sample. Shouldn't take long.' He leaned over the baby as the nurses positioned her on the table, keeping her body and legs as still as possible.

Toni swabbed the crease in the skin above the symphysis pubis with an alcohol wipe. He inserted the fine, 23-gauge needle to its full length and then drew it back, aspirating with the attached 2-ml syringe at the same time. Urine flowed into the barrel of the syringe almost immediately, and by the time Emily had gathered enough lung power to express her outrage, the procedure was virtually completed.

'Looks pretty cloudy,' Toni commented. 'I'd like a result back on this as soon as possible.'

'I'll take her back to Mum,' Mandy offered, scooping the baby up for a cuddle. 'It's the only thing that's going to cheer you up, isn't it, button?'

Toni dropped his gloves into the bin. The only thing that would cheer *him* up would be time with Pip and finding out that she *did* want a future with him. A family. But that obviously wasn't going to happen in a hurry, was it?

Maybe it would never happen.

It was no wonder they said that timing was everything. If Shona hadn't become ill when she had, things would be very different. None of those wounding words would have been uttered. It had been cool for Pip to have a boyfriend until the prospect of losing the head of their small family had been revealed. Alice could have shared a 'sister' but not a mother. And why should she? Her need for Pip's love and attention was much greater than Toni's.

It just didn't feel like that.

'Heaven's above, what's all that commotion?'

'It's all right, Mrs Evans. Try and keep still while I get this dressing in place.' The frightened twitch had been enough for paper-thin skin to slough away from the raw flesh Pip had been trying to re-cover.

'But the noise!'

There certainly was something happening in the corridor near the cubicle Mrs Evans was occupying. It sounded like a busload of children had been deposited around the waiting area for the emergency department, except they sounded far too happy to be unwell or injured.

'I'll go and see what it is in a minute. There…' Pip smoothed the wrinkles from the skin flap and reached for a dressing to hold it in place. 'You'll have to be careful of this for a while.'

'Oh, I know, dear.' Mrs Evans sighed wheezily. 'It's such a curse, having skin that tears like this. I barely touched that cabinet door.'

'It's the medication you're on that makes it like that. You've been using steroids for your breathing problems for a long time, haven't you?"

'I have a terrible chest,' Mrs Evans agreed. 'I was trying to get my puffer when I knocked my arm. Never seen so much blood! I had to call an ambulance.'

'How's your breathing feeling at the moment?"

'Terrible! I'm as tight as a drum.'

'I'll have a listen to your chest.' Pip wound a crêpe bandage over the dressing to avoid having to use anything sticky on her elderly patient's fragile skin.

The noise in the corridor had subsided but started again as Pip was trying to sort out the significance of the various wheezes and crackles she could hear in Mrs Evans's lungs. She hooked her stethoscope around her neck and slipped through the curtains to see what was going on.

The sight made her smile and it felt like the first time her lips had moved in such a direction for many days.

A procession of children in bright costumes was coming back through the double doors that led to the main reception and waiting area. They carried bags and were shouting 'Trick or treat' at regular intervals. They were obviously paediatric inpatients as a lot of staff were accompanying them and some of the children were in wheelchairs or being carried. One was in a bed decorated to look like a rowing boat and the child was waving a set of cardboard oars. He was being pushed by a pirate.

230 THE ITALIAN DOCTOR'S PERFECT FAMILY

A large pirate with a jaunty hat and a patch over one eye, who was laughing as he tried to cope with other children who wanted to be so close they were making the task of pushing the boat somewhat hazardous. Pip recognised him well before she heard him say, 'Shiver me timbers,' in that delicious accent and she had to catch her breath as she watched.

He looked to be completely in his element. Surrounded by children and enjoying every moment of it. Shona had been right, hadn't she? Toni would want to have his own children and he *should* have them. A whole tribe of them. He'd be the most amazing father.

Did he look this happy because of his small companions or was there something else that could be contributing? The fact that she was allowing him his freedom perhaps? The chance to quietly distance himself from the baggage and inadequacy she brought with her and find someone else who would be far better mother material for his own children? He looked so much happier than Pip thought she could ever feel again.

Toni must have felt her stare because he looked in her direction and her heart twisted painfully at the way his smile faded so rapidly. The way his face emptied of that happiness cut into her like a knife. Only a week ago, seeing her would have had the opposite effect on his features. Pip hadn't seen him for days now. She'd been hoping he would come down to Emergency or at least ring her.

It was proving a lot more difficult than she'd imagined, sticking to her resolve of putting Alice first and giving Toni the opportunity to escape the dramas her family situation represented. She missed him desperately and had to remind herself repeatedly that putting her own wishes first would be reinforcing Alice's impression of her selfishness. If she made any move to contact Toni it would be the thin edge of a wedge she would never be able to control. An admission of defeat. But if he contacted her, it would be different. Pip wasn't quite sure of her reasoning, she just knew it could somehow be justified. That if he thought enough of her to put up with the kind of stress her family represented, the chance of a future together would be virtually guaranteed.

He hadn't rung. Pip hadn't even received a text message to ask how she was.

'What's going on, dear?' Mrs Evans sounded querulous.

'It's Hallowe'en,' Pip said over her shoulder. 'The children's ward is having a procession. They're all dressed up.'

'Lot of nonsense,' Mrs Evans pronounced. 'And they're far too noisy. There are sick people in here.' She coughed, as if to prove her point.

'Mmm.' Pip was waiting until the procession passed her. If Toni glanced her way again, she was going to smile. To say hello. Maybe even suggest they meet for a coffee. It was too hard, this staying away from him. There had to be a way to work something out that wouldn't undermine the repair work she was trying to accomplish with her daughter.

'Trick or treat!' a small fairy said.

'Sorry, hon, I haven't got anything I can give you.'

Toni and the boat were almost level with her

now, a large island in a slow-moving sea of small children.

'Hey,' Pip called softly. 'You look like you're having a good time.'

'We are indeed.' Toni's return smile was brief. Detached. It had less warmth than a new patient would receive. Pip knew that because she'd seen that kind of introductory smile. She'd also seen the kind of smile he gave someone he loved and this one couldn't be less like it. 'How are you, Pippa?'

'I'm fine.' Such an automatic response but to say anything else would barely give lip service to the tip of the iceberg that had undermined Pip's life to such an overwhelming extent. A stressful job. A hostile daughter. A potentially broken relationship…a dying mother.

'Good.' The word was clipped. Part of an exchange that was going to be fleeting because the forward movement of the procession had not ceased. Fleeting—and painful. The few seconds of eye contact so far had been searing.

'And your mother? How is she?'

'Doing well.' For now. 'We've got her insulin levels under control.'

Toni's nod was as brief as his smile had been. 'And Alice?'

'Still not talking to me.' Pip had to blink quickly. Tears she had been holding back successfully for days were alarmingly close. 'And you? How are you, Toni?' The words were rushed. A desperate attempt to keep a line of communication open. They were too formal. Totally inadequate.

'Oh, I'm fine, too.' Toni broke the eye contact, turning his head. 'You OK, Jodi? Keeping up? Want a ride on the boat, *cara*?'

Pip's gaze followed his to the girl pushing the oxygen cylinder, who did look out of breath. Then it slid further. How many more children would need to be waited for? How much longer would Toni be this close? Was she going to have a chance to say anything else? But what *could* she say?

A nurse carrying a small tiger was bringing up the rear of the procession but Pip's eye was caught by the figure right behind the nurse.

Alice. Arriving, as arranged, for her lift home after school.

Looking as sullen and uncommunicative as

she had for the last four days. She was staring at the unusual spectacle in the corridor ahead of her and seemed to be focused on the pirate. Had she recognised Toni? Had she seen Pip and guessed that she was talking to him?

Suddenly her daughter's expression didn't strike Pip as being sullen. It was more like being desperately unhappy. When she caught her gaze, Pip smiled and waved.

Toni turned his head as though wanting to see what had caught her attention. Then he shoved the bed onwards.

'Good to see you, Pippa,' he said, without turning his head.

And then he was gone.

Pip went back to her patient. Alice knew the way to the staffroom and would be engrossed in her homework by the time Pip went to collect her. The distraction of treating a patient was exactly what Pip needed right now. Alice's timing had been perfect, hadn't it? Especially just after her realisation that Toni should have his own children—with a mother who was a lot more capable of parenting than she was.

Maybe their relationship would have foundered without the crisis in her family. Maybe Alice had done them all a favour with her pre-emptive strike.

Wishing things could be different was a waste of emotional energy and Pip was tired enough to realise her store was not inexhaustible. What strength she did have had to be reserved for her mother and her daughter. She wasn't going to let either of them down, no matter how hard it was.

'I haven't seen Toni for days,' Shona remarked. 'Must be almost a week. And you've been home every evening you're not working, Pip. What's going on?'

'Nothing.'

'Philippa!' It was exactly the tone Pip adopted with Alice when she knew the answer was way less than truthful.

Pip let out a resigned breath. 'I'm not seeing him just at the moment.'

'Why on earth not?'

'I need to show Alice she's more important than a boyfriend, I guess.'

'Is *that* what all these "no-speaks" are about? I thought it was just that shoplifting business.'

'I'm talking to Alice. She's the one who's not speaking.' Pip started clearing the table. 'At least she's not avoiding you any more, Mum.'

'Quite the opposite. She's gone all clingy. She'll be waiting for me now in the living room, I expect, wanting to show me all her homework.'

'Are you up to it? You don't want an early night?'

'I'm fine. I want to make sure she's all right. I thought she was looking a bit pale, didn't you?'

'She's been looking like that for days. Unhappy.'

'She hardly touched her dinner.'

'No. Maybe she didn't like it. Ask her if she wants a sandwich.' Pip smiled at her mother. 'How are you feeling, anyway? You're actually looking a bit brighter.'

'I'm feeling a lot better. And I intend to make the most of every moment I have left with my family, you know. Sleeping's a waste of time.' She was watching Pip rinse the plates. 'And you shouldn't waste time either. You should talk to Toni and patch things up. You can't let him think *he's* not important. Unless you've changed your mind about him.'

'No, I haven't changed my mind. I still love him. But I think it might be too late. I think he might be relieved to be away from *me*.' Pip sighed heavily. 'And it hasn't really helped with Alice. I don't seem to be able to the right thing whichever way I turn.'

'Welcome to parenthood.' Shona smiled wryly. 'Seriously, though, love—you can't put what Alice wants above what's going to make you happy. Self-sacrifice never works in the long term. It just builds resentment. It's a ticking bomb.'

'Look who's talking! How much did you give up to help me raise Alice?'

'It wasn't purely altruistic, as you well know. I did it because it made *me* happy. It gave me a reason to carry on after Dad died and…and maybe it wasn't the right thing to do.' Shona pushed her chair back, got slowly to her feet and went to hug her daughter. 'Maybe it's my fault that things are difficult between you two at present, with neither of you having the kind of relationship you should have had.'

'Don't say that, Mum.' Pip hugged her mother back, hating how thin Shona was now. 'It worked. It was a wonderful thing to do and I love you for it. And Alice adores you.'

'Yes. I've had something not many grand-mothers are blessed with, that's for sure.'

'It's just the wrong time to let someone else into my life.'

'No.' Shona almost pushed Pip away so that she could see her face. 'It's the perfect time. You can't give up on it just because Alice is disgrun-tled. On top of everything else, she's a teenager almost. She'll get over herself eventually. She loves you, Pip. She wants you to be happy.' Shona's smile was amused now. 'She just doesn't realise it yet.'

'But I can't give Toni what he wants anyway. It would never work.'

'Why not? What is it that you can't give him?'

'Children. A family.'

'What's Alice, then? Chopped liver?'

'You know what I mean. You said it yourself. He'll want his own children and I can't give him that.'

'Are you sure about that?'

What was Shona asking? Pip wondered.

Whether she might change her mind about having more children? Or whether she was sure that that was what Toni wanted in his future? How could she be so sure when they hadn't even talked about it? Hadn't talked about anything at all in days.

Pip had to close her eyes and take a deep breath to deal with the wave of misery that came with the strength of missing Toni this much.

'I guess I'm not totally sure,' she admitted finally.

'Then talk to Toni,' Shona said. 'Always talk about everything, love. It always worked for your father and me and it's the best advice I can pass on. Not talking will make a mountain out of a molehill every time.'

Maybe the mountain was finding the courage to initiate such a conversation with Toni in the first place. Or finding the time to make any contact at all.

Having thought about her mother's advice all night, Pip had come to work determined to find a way to talk to Toni. A phone call had been deemed too impersonal but when she used her break time to visit his office, she found it empty.

It was even harder to summon the courage to make another attempt. Far easier to allow herself to be swept into the controlled chaos of an unusually busy afternoon in the emergency department.

Patient after patient to see. Assessments to be made, tests ordered, results reviewed and treatments decided on and initiated. The ambulance service was being run off its feet as well. Stretcher after stretcher rolled in. People were having heart attacks and strokes. Asthma attacks and accidents.

Pip barely registered the call for a paediatric consult from the neighbouring resus bay as the department dealt with the aftermath of an MVA involving two carloads of mothers and their young children. She was looking after one of the mothers and she had barely finished her primary survey of airway, breathing and circulation adequacy when her patient screwed up her face and groaned in an alarming fashion.

'What's wrong, Stephanie?' Pip queried sharply. 'What's hurting?'

'I think…it's the baby.'

Stephanie was pregnant with her third child. Her oldest was in the next-door resus bay and sounded like he'd been concussed badly enough to warrant a specialist consult. With the pregnancy being almost full term, Pip had included a foetal check in her primary survey but there had been no sign of imminent labour and the baby's heartbeat had sounded strong and regular. Pip had been about to order an ultrasound examination in any case, because of the possibility of abdominal trauma for the mother after the driver's airbag had been deployed in the collision.

'Try not to push.' Pip was pulling on a fresh pair of gloves. 'I'll see what's going on.'

It was immediately apparent that there was a lot going on. The bed was soaked with amniotic fluid and the bulge that was about to become a baby's head was growing rapidly.

'You're right,' Pip told Stephanie. 'Your baby doesn't want to wait any longer.' She caught the attending nurse's startled gaze. 'Grab a birth kit for me, please. And some entonox.'

Stephanie groaned again and, as always, the undertone of agony triggered unpleasant memories for Pip. She knew exactly how excruciating the pain of labour could be but at least Stephanie wasn't going to have to endure hours and hours of it. By the look of how fast this labour was progressing, it could well be over before they could even set up the entonox for pain relief.

'How long did your last labour go for?'

'About an hour. *Ah-h-h*!' The sound became strangled. There was no point in asking Stephanie not to push. The force was clearly well beyond her control.

Pip held her hands ready to catch the baby. There was no time to call for assistance. Or even to check the position of the umbilical cord or use suction to clear the nasopharynx as the head emerged. It seemed that one moment the head was crowning and the next Pip was holding the slippery bundle, keeping it head down to help drain any fluid in its airways.

'Oh!' Stephanie seemed as stunned as Pip had been by the precipitous birth. 'Oh, my God! Is he all right?'

'He's a she,' Pip responded. 'You've got a little girl, Stephanie.'

The baby's warbling cry was a huge relief. An emergency department resus bay was probably not the ideal facility to resuscitate a limp newborn. There wasn't even a paediatrician within shouting distance.

Or was there? The nurse had just arrived back with the birthing kit and an entonox cylinder. Her jaw dropped.

'Can you see if anyone from Paeds has arrived next door yet?' Pip asked.

'I'm right here.' The tall figure of Toni loomed behind the nurse. 'I heard the cry. What's the Apgar score?'

'I haven't done one yet.' The baby was pinking up nicely, though. She was moving in Pip's hands and her cry was increasing steadily in volume.

'Here, let me.' Toni held out his arms. 'I'll hold her while you cut the cord.' He smiled at Stephanie. 'I love babies,' he told her.

The third stage of Stephanie's labour was not going to be as fast as the rest had been. Pip waited, running a check of Stephanie's vital signs and trying to watch Toni at the same time as he examined the baby, checking its muscle tone, heart and respiration rate, colour and movement.

'She's perfect,' he pronounced. 'We don't have any scales here so we'll weigh her as soon as we get you up to the ward.'

He wrapped the baby in a clean, fluffy towel the nurse had ready but he didn't give her back to Stephanie immediately. He stood there, the tiny baby in his arms, smiling at it.

And something inside Pip simply dissolved.

He was born to be a father, this man. And she wanted him to be able to hold his own child like that one day.

Their child?

Was it actually possible that her love for this man was strong enough for her to overcome the massive block she had set in place after Alice's birth and cemented into place a little more firmly every time she considered herself to have failed as a mother in some way? Was her reluctance really a memory blown out of all proportion because of the other circumstances surrounding it? Like being so afraid of being a mother. Of ruining her life. Alice had been a noisy, demanding, terrifying little bundle and Pip had always felt desperately out of her depth.

Maybe things would be very different now she was older. If she had a child who had a father.

If that father was Toni.

In a totally unexpected flip, Pip realised how sad it would be if Toni *didn't* want children of his own. How sad it would be if she never had the joy of seeing him hold a child of theirs like that. Of having the chance to try again as a mother after all she had learned and do things differently. Better.

As he moved to hand the infant to her mother, Toni looked up and caught Pip's gaze. She tried to smile but her lips wouldn't co-operate. They wobbled. Worse, Toni didn't even try to smile back. It was impossible to interpret the expression in those dark eyes.

Was he still upset with her?

Remembering those words that denied him the chance of having children if she was his partner?

Was there some way she could communicate, with just a look, what she was feeling right now? That her love for him was strong enough to overcome any obstacles—as long as he felt the same way?

No. There was no chance. Pip's name was being called. She turned to see that Suzie had her head through the gap in the curtains.

'What's up, Suzie?'

'There's an ambulance coming in. Twelve-year-old girl who collapsed at school.'

'You want me to take it?' Pip was puzzled. It was taking a moment to refocus on a professional level. They must be very busy if she needed to leave a patient before she could arrange transfer to the next step in her care.

'Not exactly…' Suzie bit her lip. 'I just thought you should know. I'm sorry, Pip…but it's Alice.'

CHAPTER NINE

'ON THE count of three. One, two…three.'

Pip couldn't get near Alice just yet. They were transferring her from the stretcher to the bed in Resus 4, the only highly resourced area not in use following the influx of patients from the car accidents, and the paramedic was doing the handover to the only consultant available. Toni.

'She's febrile—temperature of 39.4. Tachycardic at 120, tachypnoea at 26 and hypotensive—75 over 45. GCS 13—she's been drowsy and confused.'

'What happened at the school?'

'She started vomiting and complained of severe abdominal pain and then collapsed. Apparently unconscious for about a minute. She was rousable but confused when we arrived.'

'Keep that oxygen on,' Toni directed the

nurse. He looked at the IV line in Alice's arm. 'Is that patent?'

'Yes.'

'Fluids?'

'We've run a bolus of 500 mils 0.9 per cent saline,' the paramedic responded.

'Any change in blood pressure?'

'No.'

'Blood-glucose level?'

'Didn't get a chance to do one—sorry.'

Toni was at the head end of the bed. 'Alice? Open your eyes, *cara*. Do you know where you are?'

Alice opened her eyes but turned her head instantly and closed them again, emitting a groan that cut through Pip like a knife.

'It's OK, Alice.' Toni's voice was like a reassuring caress. It wasn't that he knew Alice—he would have been like that with any young patient. 'We're going to look after you.' He touched her cheek. 'Is it your tummy again? Is it hurting?'

The incoherent sound from Alice seemed to indicate agreement. Toni's hand went to her stomach and Pip saw the frown that coincided with another groan from Alice.

'Abdo's rigid,' he said.

This was bad. A rigid abdomen had to mean something serious. Internal bleeding or infection. Pip stepped closer as the barrier the stretcher had made between her and the bed was finally removed.

'I'm here, Alice,' she said, trying to sound calm and as reassuring as Toni had. 'It's OK, hon. You're going to be OK.' She caught the small hand lying on the bed, confident that this crisis would have done what no amount of talking had been able to do in the last few days and would have overcome the barrier Alice had erected between them. She had always turned to Pip as a mother whenever she was hurt or frightened.

But not this time.

Alice dragged her hand out of Pip's grasp. 'Go *away*,' she said clearly. 'I don't want you here.'

The paramedic at the foot end of the stretcher that was disappearing through the curtains turned to give Pip a startled glance, as though she had no right to be there. Already upset at Alice's public and very unexpected rejection, it didn't help.

'I'm her *mother*,' Pip snapped.

The paramedic shrugged, steering to one side to allow registrar Graham to enter the space.

'I don't want you here,' Alice sobbed. 'I want *Nona*.'

She was obviously becoming more distressed. Her breathing rate had increased until she was gasping between sobs. Her arms moved wildly enough to threaten the security of the IV line and Toni caught the hand before it hooked the plastic tubing coming from the bag of fluids suspended overhead.

'Take it easy, *cara*,' he said. 'It's all right. Everything's all right.'

Amazingly, Alice did start to settle, either because of Toni's words or the fact that Pip had taken a bewildered step backwards. She didn't understand. Why was Toni's attention acceptable when hers wasn't? Wasn't it Toni that Alice held at fault for the disruption to their lives? Had Pip put him at arm's length for no good reason and just suffered herself under the mistaken belief she was doing what Alice wanted?

Fear mixed with confusion took Pip back to a

response she would never normally have considered acceptable as an adult.

It wasn't fair!

'Oxygen saturation is dropping.'

Toni looked up at Graham's observation. 'Right. I want an arterial blood gas and two sets of blood cultures,' he ordered. 'And urinalysis. Full blood count, urea, creatinine, electrolytes, and a coagulation profile.' He looked at the nurse. 'Let's do a bedside BGL and a 12-lead ECG. I want a chest X-ray and someone here with a portable ultrasound machine, stat. Page a paediatric anaesthetist, too.'

He was unhooking his stethoscope as he moved around the bed to speak to Pip. He put his hand on her elbow and guided her towards the curtains.

'This looks like septic shock,' he said quietly, 'You should be prepared in case we need to put her on a ventilator.'

Alice was *that* sick? Instinctively Pip tried to move back towards her daughter but Toni's grip on her elbow tightened. His tone was apologetic.

'She's sick,' he said sympathetically, 'which

is probably why she's decided she doesn't want you here.'

'But I—'

'I know.' The hand squeezed her arm, conveying more than words could. 'But if it's upsetting her, it would be better if you weren't here just for now. I'm sorry, Pip.'

He'd called her Pip, instead of his special 'Pippa'. It didn't feel right. Toni was being so professional here. Understanding and caring but…distant. Was that why Alice was prepared to accept him treating her? Could she sense the authority and skill and lack of personal attachment under the current circumstances?

He was doing exactly what Pip was failing to do.

Toni seemed to sense what she was thinking. 'Be strong,' he said softly. 'I'll look after her.'

Pip knew that he would and his words, or perhaps just that personal encouragement, were enough to give her strength. She knew he was right. If Pip's presence was going to distress Alice further when she was already in trouble, she would be doing harm by insisting on staying. However heart-breaking it was, she had to take herself out of this. The only reason she could find that strength was in knowing that Toni would be caring for her daughter.

'Thank you,' she whispered. She cleared her throat and spoke with more certainty. 'I'll call Mum. You can tell Alice I'm sure she'll be here as soon as it's possible.'

By the time Shona arrived at the hospital, Alice was deeply unconscious in a drug-induced state to allow mechanical ventilation.

Shona gasped with shock. 'Oh, my God, what's happened to her?'

There was no need for Pip to be excluded from the area now. Her patients had all been handed to the care of other staff members and Shona needed her support. Her shocked gaze had gone from the paediatric anaesthetist, who was adjusting controls on the ventilator, to Toni, who was scrubbed and gowned and using forceps and a swab to clean the side of Alice's neck in preparation for inserting a central venous line.

'What's happening?' Shona asked in distress.

'Alice's blood pressure is still too low,' Pip told

her. 'Toni's putting a line into one of the bigger veins, which means they can administer fluid faster and also measure the pressures more accurately.'

'But why is she on a machine?'

'She's got some fluid in her lungs, which means she's not getting as much oxygen as she needs. The machine can improve that.' Pip watched as Toni felt Alice's neck with his gloved hand, identifying the carotid pulse so he could insert the needle into the internal jugular vein that ran parallel to the carotid artery.

'But why? I thought you said she had an infection.'

'She does. It's got out of hand. She's got something known as septic shock.'

'What sort of infection is it?'

'That's what we're trying to find out,' Toni said. 'Her abdomen is rigid so that's what we're focusing on right now. We're about to get a urinary catheter in place to get a specimen for analysis and we'll be doing an ultrasound examination next. Graham, have you got all the blood you need for cultures?'

'Yes.'

'We'll start antibiotics stat, then. Flucloxacillin 50 mg per kilo and Cefolaxime, also 50mg per kilo. She's about thirty-two kilos, isn't she, Pippa?'

'She was but I think she's lost a bit of weight in the last few days. She hasn't been eating well.'

'I thought she looked a bit pale last night,' Shona said. 'I asked her if she felt all right and she said yes.'

'How did she seem this morning?'

'Quiet.' It was Pip who answered this time. 'She didn't say a word to me during breakfast but that's hardly unusual at the moment.'

Nobody seemed to think the comment was strange but the staff members were concentrating on stabilising a very sick young girl.

'I'm still not happy with this blood pressure,' Toni said. 'We'll start infusion of an inotropic agent as soon as I've got this line secured.'

Dopamine, Pip thought. That's what they needed to try and get the blood pressure up. Not that she could say or do anything medical here. She was reduced to the status of a relative, nothing more. She hadn't been expected to even try finishing her shift in the emergency department. Any patients that had been under her care had been transferred by Suzie to other staff before the ambulance carrying Alice had arrived, which was just as well because Pip was in no state to treat anybody. Especially her own daughter.

'She didn't want me anywhere near her,' she had told Shona. 'She only wants you.'

'She doesn't know what she wants at the moment,' Shona had said matter-of-factly. 'We're both here for her and she knows that.'

They both stood close to the head of Alice's bed. Her eyes were shut and her mouth disfigured by the tube and mouthguard and the ties that were keeping them in place. Red-gold hair fanned out over the white pillow and the small face was almost as pale as the pillowslip.

'I can't believe this is happening,' Pip murmured. 'How could she get *this* sick this fast?'

The abdominal ultrasound gave them a provisional diagnosis.

'There's what looks like a pseudocyst here,' Toni pointed out.

'What's that?' Shona asked.

'It can be a complication of acute pancreatitis,' Toni responded. 'It's a collection of fluid and necrotic debris with the walls being formed by the pancreas and other surrounding organs. It can subside spontaneously or it can develop into an abscess. This area here…' Toni scrolled back to put another saved image onto the screen '…looks like it could be an abscess that's burst, which could explain the peritonitis and septicaemia.'

'What needs to be done?' Pip asked. 'Could that other pseudocyst be infected as well?'

'We'll do a CT scan and a guided needle aspiration. If it is the source of infection, surgery may be necessary to clean things up. In the meantime, we'll be monitoring Alice closely in the paediatric intensive care unit.'

'How long will she need to be on that machine?' Shona's anxiety was obvious.

'It depends on how well she responds to the antibiotics and what her lung function looks like. We should have a better idea in a few hours.'

Those few hours stretched into a few more. Late that evening, Alice was taken to Theatre.

Pip, Shona and Toni accompanied the entourage as far as the theatre anteroom, where the anaesthetist and surgeon were waiting.

'The good news,' the surgeon said, 'is that we'll be able to do the division of the sphincter of Oddi at the same time, which should make sure nothing like this happens again. Toni, do you want to come in and observe?'

'Yes. I'm on call but I don't think I have any other patients who will need me for a while.'

'Give your pager to one of the nurses. They can take any calls.'

Pip bent over the still unconsciousness Alice. She blinked back tears as she smoothed tendrils of fine hair from her daughter's forehead and kissed her gently.

'See you soon, hon,' she whispered. 'Love you.'

Pip and Shona went back to the ICU to wait. Shona eventually fell asleep in the armchair beside Alice's empty bed. Pip paced until the night staff took pity on her, made her hot chocolate and suggested she try to watch a late movie on the television in the unoccupied relatives' room.

'It might distract you for a bit. We'll come and let you know the second we hear anything.'

But it wasn't the night staff who came to find Pip later as she sat staring at a blank television screen, her hot drink forgotten and cold. It was Toni.

'It went well,' he said as he sank wearily into the chair beside hers. 'Everybody's happy. She's in Recovery for the moment but they'll bring her back here soon.'

Pip started to get up. 'I'll go and tell Mum.'

Toni put his hand on her arm. 'Shona's asleep. I checked when I went looking for you. It might be a good idea to let her have a few minutes more rest, yes?'

Pip nodded and sat back again. 'I still can't believe this is happening,' she said slowly. 'We're not out of the woods yet, are we?'

'We'll get there.' Toni's voice had that same reassuring note he had used with Alice when she'd arrived in the ED. 'She's stable. Her blood pressure has come up a little and there's no deterioration in her lung function. We've just got to be patient and give the antibiotics a chance to get on top of things.' He rubbed his temple with his fingers and closed his eyes for a moment.

'You're tired,' Pip observed. 'You wouldn't be here all night like this if it wasn't Alice, would you?'

'I am on call.' A half-smile appeared. 'But even if I wasn't, I would be here, Pippa. For you.'

'I don't deserve your support. And I don't blame you for being angry with me. For wanting out.'

Toni opened his mouth as though to protest, but Pip didn't give him the chance.

'I thought I was doing the right thing. That it wasn't the right time for us to talk. That I shouldn't be putting any pressure on you if you didn't want to be there.'

Toni opened his mouth but again, he didn't get the chance to say anything as the words spilled from Pip.

'The only thing I could do was try and repair the damage as far as Alice and I were concerned, but nothing helped. I don't think it would have made any difference if you'd still been around or not. I've never done the right thing as far as

Alice goes.' Pip sighed unhappily. 'I don't think I've ever been a good mother.'

'You're a wonderful mother,' Toni said with conviction, as Pip finally paused. 'I watched you with Alice when she was going into Theatre. I think that even unconscious she would have been aware of your love. It filled the room.' His smile was poignant now. 'I would have given anything to have my mother feel like that about me. I would have forgiven every forgotten birthday, every lonely night…everything.'

'Alice isn't about to forgive me. I feel like I've failed her. This shouldn't be happening. She must have been feeling unwell for days. I noticed she was pale and not eating much and I put it down to her being so angry with me. How self-centred was that?'

'You can't blame yourself.'

Pip ignored the comfort. 'I was always self-centred. I let Mum take over caring for her when she was a baby because it all seemed too hard.'

'You were sixteen. No more than a child yourself.'

'I was so scared of her,' Pip admitted with a

rueful smile. 'I couldn't even bath her because I was scared I'd drop her or drown her or something. She screamed every time I tried to dress her. It was weeks before I could even get her to take her bottle when I was holding it. We used to both sit there and cry.'

Toni took hold of Pip's hand. 'Wasn't there someone there to help you?'

'Of course. Mum was there for me every minute. Alice wouldn't have survived otherwise.' She loved the fact that Toni was there with her. Touching her. Holding her hand. But he'd probably be doing this for any distraught mother with a child in the intensive care unit, wouldn't he?

'No, I mean professional help. Your family doctor or someone.'

'I didn't have postnatal depression or anything. I just couldn't cope.'

'Are you sure about that? Sounds like it was a pretty miserable experience.'

Pip was silent for a moment. 'I've never thought of that, even with the hindsight of medical training. When I have thought of that time, I decided I had made it the way it was. I felt like I'd failed Alice from the moment I found out I was pregnant. I hated it. The way people stared at me—knowing they knew far more about my private life than I wanted them to. I hated being fat but then I wanted to stay that way for ever because I was so terrified of actually *having* the baby. It must have contributed to the bad labour.'

'It was really bad?'

'Horrendous. I had a midwife who didn't think much of teenage mothers. She told me to toughen up. That people had babies all the time without making the kind of fuss I was making. That I'd had my fun and now I could grow up and deal with the consequences.'

'That's appallingly unprofessional.'

'That's what the consultant thought when he was finally called in, thanks to Mum's demands. I'd been in labour for about fourteen hours by then and I got terribly sick on entonox.'

'The woman should have been fired.'

'I think she was. Or she resigned when Mum made a formal complaint afterwards. The doctor was furious. I had marginal cephalopelvic disproportion. A trial labour shouldn't have gone for more than about four hours. It was too late for a Caesarean by then but the forceps delivery was dreadful and I ended up going to Theatre anyway. I had a post-partum haemorrhage and lost so much blood I needed a transfusion. I didn't even see Alice for three days.'

'Hardly the best start to something you weren't ready for anyway.'

'I was so sure I could never face it again. I avoided childbirth during my training as much as I could. Even hearing the pain Stephanie was in today was enough to send a shiver down my spine.'

Toni was still holding her hand. His thumb traced a gentle circle on her palm. 'I saw the way you were looking at that baby,' he said slowly. 'You looked...very sad.'

'Did I?' Pip had been trying to communicate the breakthrough in the way she felt about having another child. What message had Toni received? She had been sad for a second, though, hadn't she? Thinking about never having the opportunity to see him holding his own baby. *Her* baby. 'You looked so happy, Toni.' Pip couldn't help smiling. 'You were born to be a father, I think.'

'I would like to have my own family more than anything,' Toni agreed. His hand tightened on Pip's. 'But—'

The door to the relatives' room opening cut off what he was about to say.

'Alice is on her way down,' the nurse informed them. 'And Shona's awake. She's asking where you are, Pip.'

What had Toni been about to say? Was he going to qualify his wishes by suggesting that Pip could be part of his future without having to give birth again? That they could adopt children or not have any at all? Or perhaps that he loved her but he understood that it was enough to make their relationship unworkable and therefore he would have to keep searching to find the mother for his children?

There had been no opportunity for Pip to explain how she'd really felt when she'd seen him holding Stephanie's baby. That miraculous hope that she could put her past behind her and move on to a new life in more ways than one.

Right now, part of her past and her future was pulling her in. All Pip's emotional energy had to be spent supporting Alice. If Toni was right, and there was even a possibility that Alice was aware of her love, then her daughter was going to have it—in spades—whether she was awake and responsive or not.

With the resilience of youth and the aid of antibiotics, Alice's condition improved steadily over the next twelve hours. Her blood pressure crept up until it was within normal limits and the function of vital organs like her kidneys and lungs became acceptable enough to consider taking her off the ventilator.

Armed with a new sheaf of test results, Toni was making his way back to the intensive care unit early the next afternoon. Despite his lack of sleep, he had just completed a full ward round and was impatient to get back to the unit and pass on the good news. Annoyingly, the lift doors reopened before any upward movement but the latecomer was none other than Alice's grandmother.

'I went home for a few things,' Shona told Toni. 'Pip thought Alice might like her own pyjamas and music and old Ted.' She showed him a battered soft toy on the top of the items in the bag she held.

Toni hit the button for the third floor. 'I'm just on my way up to see Alice myself. The last blood tests are looking much better. I think we'll be able to take her off the ventilator this afternoon and let her wake up.'

'Oh, that's wonderful!' For a moment the deep lines of anxiety on Shona's face relaxed, leaving her looking drained and exhausted.

'How are you holding up, Shona?'

'I'm OK.'

'Really?'

Shona smiled at the undercurrent of doubt in his tone. 'Really.' She patted his arm. 'I think I'll be around for a while yet, Toni.'

'I certainly hope so.'

'Yes.' Shona adjusted her hold on the bag. 'My girls still need me for a bit, I think.'

'Of course they do.'

'Not that I'm afraid of dying. Love has an

amazing power to conquer fear.' Shona was watching the numbers change on the lift floor display. 'I believe my spirit is going to connect with Jack's somehow. I've been missing him for thirteen years now, you know.'

'You must have loved each other very much.'

Shona smiled again. A very private smile. She said nothing as the lift doors opened but gave Toni a very direct glance as they stepped out.

'You look tired,' she said. 'Did you get any sleep last night?'

'Not much.'

'Have you eaten?'

'Kind of.'

'You need to look after yourself, Toni.' The instruction was issued with all the sternness any mother would summon. Then she softened the tone. 'My girls need you, too, you know, even if Alice doesn't realise it yet.'

Toni stopped by the central desk in the unit to collect Alice's notes as Shona went behind the glass wall that screened the area Alice occupied. He saw her hug Pip and then bend to kiss Alice. She took the teddy bear from the bag and tucked it gently under the covers so that Alice's arm was over the toy.

For a moment it was hard to concentrate on filing the new test results and checking his conclusions on Alice's progress.

Toni had been initially drawn into his relationship with Pip partly due to curiosity. He'd wanted to know why this small family unit worked when, on the surface, it had appeared to mirror some of the dysfunction of his own upbringing.

Now he knew what the difference was. The strength of the bond between the three generations of Murdoch women that held them together was love. A kind of love he had never had himself and had always wanted.

Marrying Pip would include him in that family. He would have a mother caring for him in the way Shona had just demonstrated she did. Sadly, it might not be for long but Toni would treasure every gesture.

He would gladly become a father for Alice. He could cope with any of the flak generated by any adjustments she needed to make in attitude and he knew they would win through in the end.

Both were compelling factors but they paled in comparison to the real reason Toni wanted to marry Pip. The insight he'd gained from their conversation last night had been enough to dismiss any lingering hurt from recent days. He understood why it was impossible for Pip to face the prospect of motherhood again. He'd seen the sadness in her face when she'd seen him holding that baby and realised it could be because she knew how important he'd always considered having his own children to be and that was something she didn't feel capable of giving him. Had allowing Alice to force the break in their relationship at least partly been due to that belief?

He had to find a way to tell her she was wrong. Yes, he had wanted his own children. To be able to give them the kind of love the Murdoch family possessed. The kind he'd never had. But there was another kind of love that was even more powerful and that was what Toni wanted more than anything else.

He wanted to love Pippa. And to have her love him back.

CHAPTER TEN

ALICE was asleep.

Peacefully asleep, without the aid of sedation. The wires and tubes connecting her to the life support equipment had been left behind in the intensive care unit when Alice had been transferred to the paediatric ward a few hours ago.

Toni was somewhere on the ward, too, despite it being well past his expected working hours today. A case of suspected meningitis in a two-year-old girl had been rushed in and he was doing the lumbar puncture and supervising the start of an antibiotic regime himself. He'd been gone for nearly an hour and during that time the lights had been dimmed and the ward had settled into a relatively calm period. A time for rest and maintenance. A time to heal or prepare for what a new day would bring.

Shona was asleep in the armchair by the window but Pip sat on a much less comfortable chair pulled up right against Alice's bed. She held her daughter's hand as she slept and watched the steady drip of the fluid keeping a forearm vein open, ready to administer her continued antibiotics or more pain relief if Alice chose to press the button of the attached pump.

The small fingers tightened a little as Alice stirred in her sleep and Pip squeezed them gently. As tired as she was, she had no desire to sleep herself. She wanted to enjoy this feeling of peace. Of knowing that the crisis for Alice was over and that when she'd woken up that afternoon, she had accepted Pip's presence as automatically as that of her grandmother. Her rejection of Pip appeared to have been forgotten.

Had being with her for every minute of this ordeal made a difference? Maybe, as Toni thought, Alice had been somehow aware it had been Pip caring for her alongside the medical staff. Smoothing salve onto dry lips, wiping her face gently with a warm, damp cloth. Talking to her. Singing endless repetitions of the 'Ottipuss' song.

Pip was humming it again now, which was enough to prevent the faint, fractious wail of a baby somewhere on the ward disturbing the bubble of contentment this private room contained. She was into the second chorus when Alice's eyes opened.

'Hi, hon.' Pip smiled. 'How are you feeling?'

'OK, I guess.'

'Are you sore? Do you need any medicine?'

'My tummy hurts a bit.'

'Press the button there. It'll give you some more morphine.'

'Will that make me go to sleep again?'

'Probably, but that's a good thing. You need to sleep so that you can rest and give your body the chance to get better.'

'*Am* I going to get better, Mummy?'

'Of course you are, hon. Really fast.'

'I thought I was going to die. Like Nona.'

'No.' Pip wound her fingers tightly over Alice's. 'You're going to be fine. And the operation you've had means that you probably won't ever get those sore tummies again.'

'Is Nona still going to die?'

'Not for a while, I hope. She's feeling quite a lot better at the moment. We'll look after her.'

'Where is she?'

'Asleep. In the chair over there by the window.'

'Where's Toni?''

'He's here somewhere. There was a sick little girl he had to go and see.'

'I'm a sick little girl.'

'This one's a lot sicker than you are now. She needed him. I expect he'll come and see you again before he goes home. He's been taking very good care of you.'

'I don't really hate him, you know.'

'I know.'

'You didn't have to stop going out with him.'

'I was trying to make things better for you.'

'Will you go out with him again?'

'I don't know.'

'Don't you *want* to go out with him again?'

Pip was silent for a moment. Alice was still a child in many ways. And for the first time, thanks to the trauma of the last few weeks, Alice felt completely *her* child. Somehow, during this period, Shona had relinquished her role of being

Alice's mother and, miraculously, Pip seemed to have stepped into the breach without failing as much as she'd thought she had.

There was still the extra dimension to their relationship, however. The friendly 'sister' component. And Pip could see that as a positive thing now. It would give them a closeness not many mothers would have with their daughters. Even so, how much should she tell her?

What was it Toni had said that time? That you have to do what feels right as a parent and that you can only do your best.

'I don't want to go out with Toni at the moment if it means that I'm going to fight with you, Alice,' she said finally. 'I want home to be the best place. For all of us.'

'But do you *want* to? Are you in love with him?'

'Yes. I do love Toni, hon. Not the same way I love you. It's completely different but very, very special.'

'I'm sorry I was so awful about it. I didn't really mean it, you know, about the babies and stuff. I think it would be cool. I'd be like another mother, wouldn't I?'

'You sure would. You'd be almost the age I was when I had you.'

'So you will marry him, then? And have babies?'

'I don't know, hon. He might not want to go out with me any more.'

'Why *not*?' Even in her increasingly drowsy state, Alice's tone held an indignation that made Pip smile. How could she have doubted the strength of love Alice had for her?

'I think I hurt his feelings when I agreed that it would be a good idea if we didn't see each other at the moment.'

'You mean it was his idea?'

'Yes.' Pip tried to banish the conviction that it would have come eventually, anyway. That Toni didn't feel the same way. She didn't want Alice to know how sad that made her. 'He understands that I've got other things in my life that are very important.'

'Like me?' Was it Pip's imagination or was there a satisfied note in Alice's voice? The knowledge that she was important enough to have been put first.

'Like you,' Pip agreed. 'But there *are* some

other things we need to talk about.' Like those babies Alice might be a second mother to.

A quiet sound from near the window made Pip realise her mother was awake and had been listening.

'You should do that, then,' Shona said. 'Go and talk to him.'

'I will,' Pip responded. 'He's busy at the moment and it's getting late. I'll do it as soon as I get the chance.'

'And you'll tell him that you're in love with him?' Alice said.

'Yes.'

Shona hadn't been the only person to hear Pip's conversation with Alice. Toni had to swallow hard to clear the lump in his throat when he'd paused to listen to Pippa singing to her daughter at this quiet end of the ward.

And then he'd waited, not wanting to interrupt that first proper conversation she'd been able to have with her daughter since she'd become so ill.

But he couldn't wait any longer. Not after hearing that admission that she intended to tell him she loved him. She *loved* him. His heart singing, he moved to step into Alice's room.

His smile was a little embarrassed. 'I couldn't help overhearing,' he lied. Then his gaze fastened on Pip. 'Would now be a good time for that talk, do you think?'

Alice's grin was weak but much more like her old self. 'You are so busted,' she told her mother.

'I guess I am.' But Pip didn't care. In the pale gleam of the nightlight in Alice's room, she could still clearly see the way Toni was looking at her.

'Go,' Shona ordered. 'I'll be here with Alice.'

Toni wasn't looking at Pip any longer. 'Is that all right with you, Alice?'

'Sure. But you'll come back, won't you, Mum?'

'Of course I will.'

Shona waved her hand at the couple as Pip slowly walked towards the door and took Toni's outstretched hand.

'Play nicely, children,' she said.

And Alice giggled.

'She's sounding so much better.'

'Isn't she? It's like the clock's been turned

back. To before she started having those attacks. Before Mum got sick.'

'To before we started seeing each other?'

'Except that I think she sees you as part of the picture now.'

'Is that what you want, Pippa?' Toni's hand pulled her to a stop near the lifts where their aimless wandering had taken them. 'Do you want me as part of *your* picture?'

The lift doors were open and, by tacit consent, they both stepped inside. Toni pushed the button to close the doors. He looked at Pip.

'Yes.' Pip felt shy because she knew Toni had overheard her telling Alice that she was in love with him but she didn't know if he felt the same way. Then, having made herself vulnerable to that extent, she knew she may as well go the whole distance. 'You're so much part of the picture I want, Toni. You make it bigger. Clearer. The colours brighter. It even has a frame that makes it perfect.'

'Not a solid frame, I hope?'

Pip could have basked for ever in the look she was receiving. It was so warm. So full of…love.

'Why not?'

'Because we might want to make that picture bigger.'

Pip's heart skipped a beat. 'You mean…with our own children?'

'No.' Toni shook his head quickly. 'I would never ask you to do something that frightened you too much, Pippa. Or something that you really didn't want to do. It's enough for me to be with you. Knowing that we have our whole lives to add to that picture. Places to go. Things to share.'

'Do you mean you don't *want* children?'

'I mean I want *you* more, *cara*. There's no one else I would want to be the mother of my children so if I don't have you, I will have nothing. You must know how much I love you.'

'You…*love* me?' The words caused a peculiar tingle that coursed through Pip. She had never felt anything like this. Like liquid hope. Or joy.

Toni was looking perplexed. 'Of course I love you. I've told you many times. Ever since that first night we spent together when you made me burn my spaghetti sauce.'

'Oh…' Maybe the meaning of those sexy,

foreign phrases hadn't been as clear as Pip had believed. 'You told me that in Italian?'

'Did I? I don't remember. Maybe. I was speaking from my heart, not my head. I thought you understood.'

'Maybe I did,' Pip confessed, 'but what's said in bed can sometimes be...not the real thing.'

'I never say anything in bed I don't mean.'

Toni's touch as he pulled her close to him was as convincing as his words. The strength of the love Pip felt for Toni was enough to render her speechless for a moment, but it didn't matter because he was still talking. Pip could feel as well as hear the low rumble of his words as she revelled in the closeness of their embrace.

'I love all of you, Pippa. Not just your beautiful body or your clever mind. I love the way you love your mother and your daughter. And if Alice will allow me to be a father to her, I will be honoured, but it's *you* I love, Pippa Murdoch—with all my heart and soul. It's you I want to marry and spend the rest of my life with.' He bent his head and kissed Pip's lips. 'I've missed you so much, my love. These last few days have felt like months.' He kissed her again.

The lift doors chose that moment to open. A startled-looking cleaner had to stop the forward movement of his polishing machine.

'Sorry,' Toni said firmly. 'This lift is occupied.' He pushed the button to close the doors again and then hit a random floor number so the lift started moving upwards.

'Now, where we were?' he murmured. 'Ah, yes. I think I was asking you to marry me, Pippa.'

'Were you?' Pip couldn't help trying to spin this delicious moment out just a little longer.

'Most definitely.'

Pip had to wait for another kiss to finish before hearing the words that thrilled her even more than she could have expected.

'Will you marry me, Pippa? Will you be my love? My wife? And let me love you for the rest of my life?'

'Yes.' Pip didn't bother trying to blink away the tears of joy that sprang to her eyes. 'I love you, too, Toni. And I love that you think I'm enough for you without having to be a mother again.'

'You are.'

'But I *want* to be the mother of your children.' Pip would have had to brush away tears that were now rolling down the side of her nose except that Toni was doing it for her. Cradling her face with both hands and using his thumbs to dry her tears. 'I want to have your babies, Toni. I want you to be a father. *Us* to be a whole family.'

The smile lit up his face. 'You really *want* that? After all you went through with Alice?'

'I love you enough to make me brave,' Pip said softly. 'If I have you with me, I can do anything.'

Toni kissed her yet again. Slowly. Tenderly. 'You have your mother's incredible strength, Pippa,' he said eventually. 'She told me that love has the power to conquer fear. She said she wasn't afraid to die because of the love she shared with your father.'

'She told me something, too.'

The lift was moving downwards again but Toni didn't seem to notice. 'What was that?'

'That it would be nice if she could plan for a wedding instead of a funeral.'

'She will,' Toni avowed. 'And maybe she'll still be with us for long enough to welcome a new grandchild.'

'It's possible.' Pip would remember this moment of hope and hang onto it for as long as she could. 'But, just to be on the safe side, do you think we should get married soon?'

'The sooner, the better.'

The lift doors opened and the cleaner was still standing with his machine on the floor they'd left, his foot tapping impatiently.

Not that Toni or Pip noticed. Wrapped in each other's arms, their kiss advertised the promise of future dreams and it firmly excluded the rest of the world.

The cleaner sighed wearily and hauled his heavy machine backwards so he could change direction and head for a different lift.

Clearly, his preferred choice was not going to be available for quite some time.

 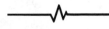

MEDICAL™

Large Print

Titles for the next six months…

January

SINGLE DAD, OUTBACK WIFE	Amy Andrews
A WEDDING IN THE VILLAGE	Abigail Gordon
IN HIS ANGEL'S ARMS	Lynne Marshall
THE FRENCH DOCTOR'S MIDWIFE BRIDE	Fiona Lowe
A FATHER FOR HER SON	Rebecca Lang
THE SURGEON'S MARRIAGE PROPOSAL	Molly Evans

February

THE ITALIAN GP'S BRIDE	Kate Hardy
THE CONSULTANT'S ITALIAN KNIGHT	Maggie Kingsley
HER MAN OF HONOUR	Melanie Milburne
ONE SPECIAL NIGHT…	Margaret McDonagh
THE DOCTOR'S PREGNANCY SECRET	Leah Martyn
BRIDE FOR A SINGLE DAD	Laura Iding

March

THE SINGLE DAD'S MARRIAGE WISH	Carol Marinelli
THE PLAYBOY DOCTOR'S PROPOSAL	Alison Roberts
THE CONSULTANT'S SURPRISE CHILD	Joanna Neil
DR FERRERO'S BABY SECRET	Jennifer Taylor
THEIR VERY SPECIAL CHILD	Dianne Drake
THE SURGEON'S RUNAWAY BRIDE	Olivia Gates

MILLS & BOON®
Pure reading pleasure

1207 LP 2P P1 Medical

MEDICAL™

Large Print

April

THE ITALIAN COUNT'S BABY	Amy Andrews
THE NURSE HE'S BEEN WAITING FOR	Meredith Webber
HIS LONG-AWAITED BRIDE	Jessica Matthews
A WOMAN TO BELONG TO	Fiona Lowe
WEDDING AT PELICAN BEACH	Emily Forbes
DR CAMPBELL'S SECRET SON	Anne Fraser

May

THE MAGIC OF CHRISTMAS	Sarah Morgan
THEIR LOST-AND-FOUND FAMILY	Marion Lennox
CHRISTMAS BRIDE-TO-BE	Alison Roberts
HIS CHRISTMAS PROPOSAL	Lucy Clark
BABY: FOUND AT CHRISTMAS	Laura Iding
THE DOCTOR'S PREGNANCY BOMBSHELL	Janice Lynn

June

CHRISTMAS EVE BABY	Caroline Anderson
LONG-LOST SON: BRAND-NEW FAMILY	Lilian Darcy
THEIR LITTLE CHRISTMAS MIRACLE	Jennifer Taylor
TWINS FOR A CHRISTMAS BRIDE	Josie Metcalfe
THE DOCTOR'S VERY SPECIAL CHRISTMAS	Kate Hardy
A PREGNANT NURSE'S CHRISTMAS WISH	Meredith Webber

MILLS & BOON®
Pure reading pleasure

1207 LP 2P P2 Medical